the

no wheel

NATALIA,

HOLD ONTO

THE WHEEL!

James Mayo

there is no wheel

james maxey

Published by:
Word Balloon Books
618 Miller Road
Hillsborough, NC 27278

ISBN-13: 978-1499139914

ISBN-10: 1499139918

Cover Design and all illustrations by James Maxey

Second printing

For Cheryl Morgan

There may not be a wheel
but there is most certainly a ring.

Publication Credits

"Introduction: A Junkie to the Max" © Edmund R. Schubert, 2011; used by permission.

"Secret Origin Essays" © James Maxey 20104

"To the East, A Bright Star" first appeared in *Asimov's*, December 2005

"Silent as Dust" first appeared in *Orson Scott Card's Intergalactic Medicine Show*, January 2008

"Final Flight of the Blue Bee" first appeared in *Asimov's*, April/May 2006

"Empire of Dreams and Miracles" first appeared in *Empire of Dreams and Miracles: The Phobos SF Anthology*, edited by Orson Scott Card and Keith Olexa, 2002

"Return to Sender" first appeared in *Orson Scott Card's Intergalactic Medicine Show*, January 2010

"Pentacle on His Forehead, Lizard on His Breath" first appeared in *Modern Magic*, the anthology, edited by W.H. Horner, August 2005

"To Know All Things That Are in the Earth" first appeared in *Orson Scott Card's Intergalactic Medicine Show*, January 2007

"Echo of the Eye" first appeared in *The Blotter*, April 2009

"Where Their Worm Dieth Not" first appeared in *Masked*, the anthology, edited by Lou Anders, 2010

"Perhaps the Snail" first appeared in *The Urban Bizarre*, the anthology, edited by Nick Mamatas, January 2004

Table of Contents

INTRODUCTION: A JUNKIE TO THE MAX
By Edmund R. Schubert
ഇൻൣൟൣഇൻൣഇൻ

I'VE BEEN A HUGE, vocal fan of James Maxey's stories for a long time now. If you've been to any science fiction convention where I've spoken on panels, you've inevitably heard me talk about James's work and how much I admire it. Heck, three of the stories in this collection I bought and published in *Orson Scott Card's Intergalactic Medicine Show*, and my only complaint is that I didn't get first look at more of them.

One of these stories ("Silent As Dust") I got to read an early draft of (somewhat by accident), and when I asked James about its status, he informed me that it was already submitted to another publication. However, he graciously added that if they rejected it, I would be next on the list of places to send it to. This caused a small black hole of despair to open up in my stomach because it was a brilliant story and there was no way any editor in their right mind would reject it. I really wanted it for *IGMS* and I wasn't going to get it.

Imagine my surprise when the story showed up in my email a few weeks later. You can also imagine my total lack of surprise when, after appearing in *IGMS*, "Silent As Dust" ended up reprinted in one the Year's Best anthologies the following year. The only thing I can say in that other editor's defense is that sometimes a story just isn't right for a particular publication. There are

i

certain stories in this collection that I couldn't have bought for *IGMS* because of our PG-13 guidelines. One thing about James: he pushes boundaries, and he pushes them *hard*.

That's one of the things I like about James's stories though; he's not afraid to push, to delve, to explore dark territory. And he doesn't pursue shock value for its own sake; he simply has an insatiable fascination with flawed characters. Actually, "flawed" doesn't begin to scratch the surface. More like seriously, tragically, deeply, mesmerizingly, painfully *fucked up* characters.

These characters often make those on the Jerry Springer show seem like sane, rational people, and the first inclination is to watch them with the same wide-eyed, carnival freak-show mentality. The difference is that with James's characters, you quickly discover that you can't help but relate to and feel for them. They're real people who made/make bad choices, or had bad choices made for them (or inflicted on them, as the case may be), and now those characters are dealing with the aftermath. And who can't relate to that? Who among us isn't dealing with the aftermath of bad choices, whether our own or someone else's—or worse yet, some horrible combination of the two?

And to me that's the source of the power and the magic in James's writing. I could talk about his gorgeous prose and his spot-on dialogue and his blah blah blah, but in the final analysis, it's his ability to make me like and root for characters without necessarily needing for them to change who they fundamentally are that raises the bar of his work above so much other short fiction. I can embrace these characters the way they are. I can look at their flaws and say "There but for the grace of God go I, because they're really *not that much* farther down the fucked up path than me and a lot of people I know."

James's stories require a strong mind and strong stomach. They're freaky weird and hauntingly honest at the same time. They'll get you as high as the drugs many of his characters use and prove to be twice as addicting.

You're going to love them.

You're going to want more.

Then you're going to need more. Yes, you will.

The good news is that you've got ten serious hits in this collection. The better news is that you can inhale them as deeply as you like and they'll be just as potent the second time around.

The bad news—and I say this from personal experience—is that after a while you *will* start craving more.

Oh yes, you will, I promise you.

Yeah. Good luck with that...

TO THE EAST, A BRIGHT STAR
ဪဪဪဪဪဪဪ

THERE WAS A SHARK in the kitchen. The shark wasn't huge, maybe four feet long, gliding across the linoleum toward the refrigerator. Tony stood motionless in the knee-deep water of the dining room. The Wolfman said the only sharks that came in this far were bull sharks, which were highly aggressive. Tony leaned forward cautiously and shut the door to the kitchen. He'd known the exact time and date of his death for most of his adult life. With only hours to go, he wasn't about to let the shark do something ironic.

Tony waded back to the living room. Here in the coolest part of the house, always shaded, he kept his most valuable possession in an ice-chest stashed beneath the stairs. He pulled away the wooden panel and retrieved the red plastic cooler. Inside was his cigar box, wrapped in plastic bags. He took the box, grabbed one of the jugs of rainwater cooling in the corner, and headed up the stairs to the bathroom. He climbed out the window above the tub onto the low sloping roof over the back porch.

Everything was damp from yesterday's rain. He took out the silver case with his last three cigarettes. He went through five matches before he got one lit. He sucked down the stale smoke as a tiny voice in his head chided him about quitting.

Tony wished the tiny voice would consult a calendar. It was a bit late to worry about cancer.

The sky shimmered with brilliant blue, not a cloud in it. The Wolfman had thought Tony was crazy to gamble on this day being clear. It had rained 200 days last year. A decade ago a comet had hit Antartica, melting half the ice cap, pumping countless tons of water vapor into the atmosphere. Cloudless skies were only a memory. And yet, in Tony's imagination, the sky of the last day had always been crystal clear. It pleased him that reality and imagination overlapped at last.

A slight breeze set waves gently lapping at the tumbled roofs and walls that lay in all directions. This had been a nice old neighborhood full of Victorian houses before the earthquakes started. Now only a few homes remained, twisted and strangely beautiful, half submerged in a shallow green ocean, surrounded by the salt-poisoned skeletons of trees still stretching toward that amazing blue sky.

"Here's to a gorgeous day," he said, raising his water jug toward the sun. He brought the jug to his lips and chugged down half a gallon in careless gulps, the water running from the corners of his mouth, dripping down to soak his shirt. He no longer saw any point in being careful with fresh water. It felt good to be wasteful again.

His thirst sated, Tony capped the jug, walked to the edge of the roof, and dropped the water into his boat. He steadied himself, turned around, held his hands over his head, then flipped backward. He landed on his feet in the center of the aluminum skiff, his arms stretched for balance as the craft gently rocked.

"So what do you think, *Pop?*" he asked, imagining his father had been watching.

Tony knew exactly what Pop would think.

"The bit with the boat, just a gimmick," Tony answered, his voice taking on a touch of an Italian accent. "And the back flip... *sloppy*. The people want *form*."

"Whatever," Tony said, his voice once more his own. The old bastard never had a kind word for him. Or even a truthful one. Last year he'd met up with Pete Pyro the Fire King over at the Dixie.

"God Hell," Pete had stammered when he finally recognized him. "Rico told me you'd gone and died of AIDS."

Which had indicated to Tony that his father wasn't open to the idea of eventual reconciliation. But what the hell. There are only so many days in a life. You can't get around to everything.

Tony untied the rope and pushed the boat away from the house. Taking up oars, he maneuvered through the submerged streets. The sun beat down with a terrible force. It was two hours before sunset. Normally, he never went out during the day. When it wasn't raining, it could reach higher than the old dial thermometer back at the house could measure, and it had marks to one hundred ten. But the whole show ended only an hour after dark, and it would take a little while to reach the old Dixie Hotel, the tallest building still standing downtown. From its roof, he'd be maybe sixty feet higher than he would have been back at his house. Not much, but there was something in him which still craved heights. The higher he could get, the better the show.

Except for the splash and creak of oars, the world was silent. It had been almost a year since he'd seen a bird, three weeks since he'd had to hide from a helicopter, and six days since the Wolfman had changed his mind and headed west. He'd gone in search of the government shelter near Black Mountain, with hydroponic gardens, nuclear power, the works.

"I hear if you put all them tunnels end to end, they cover four hundred miles," the Wolfman had said. "There's room for one more."

Tony shook his head. At best there were cold little cages for crazy people, or cripples, or junkies. The Wolfman was a little of all three. Tony missed him.

Ahead loomed the islands of rubble that marked the downtown. Rusted steel beams were tangled together in great heaps, and mirrored glass gleamed beneath the surface of the sea. The Dixie rose above all this, six stories of old red brick that had somehow survived the quakes, the flooding, and the terrible unending heat. A month ago, the Dixie had been a noisy place, a Mecca for those left behind by accident or choice. He and the Wolfman had come here often. They'd survived the last few years by scavenging, and the Dixie had been a place to trade canned goods and batteries for booze and fresh vegetables. Some old geezer named Doc had filled the upper floors of the Dixie with potted plants, and his horticultural prowess provided garden goodies all year round. Also, Doc had rigged up a distillery for fresh water, plus another for booze. He'd been king of his little world, one of the last defenders of the good life, while it lasted.

A month ago the helicopters had come and taken everyone, whether they wanted to go or not. They'd smashed the stills and tossed plants into the ocean and Tony still couldn't see the sense in it. He and the Wolfman had steered clear of the place since, in case the helicopters came back. Now it would be safe. There would be no search and rescue at this late hour.

He tied off his boat on the east side, in the shade. A steady breeze was blowing in from the north, taking the teeth out of the heat. He gulped thirstily from the water jug, pouring what was left over his face and hair. He pulled off his sweat-soaked shirt and tossed it into the sea. He untied the tarp, and unfolded a fresh cotton shirt he'd saved for this occasion. He picked up his boombox with its missing left speaker cover and pushed in fresh batteries. Over the years he'd traded away most of the CD's he'd found, keeping only a copy of *All Hail West Texas* by the Mountain Goats, a scratched-up double CD set of Mozart, and a K-Tel collection of Disco Hits. He still hadn't made up his mind what he was going to play.

Finally, he unwrapped the four layers of trash bags from the humidor. The box's contents would make all of his efforts worthwhile. He stepped through a window, into a shadowy room ankle-deep in brine. The Dixie moaned like a giant bassoon as the wind rushed through the open windows.

The stairs creaked with each step. Emptied of its people, the Dixie seemed haunted. A place he associated with life and light now sat dark and dead, the air foul with rot. No doubt the place had moaned and creaked just as loudly on his past visits, but then the sounds were masked with laughter and talk and...

He stopped. Was the wind making that sound?

He climbed three more steps.

Crying. Someone was crying, somewhere above.

He crept up to the next landing. There was no doubt now. "Hello?" he called out.

The crying stopped short.

"Hello?" he called again.

A woman began shouting, in a rapid, nearly unintelligible rush of syllables and sobs. He followed the sound, racing up two flights of stairs. He rushed past open doors, drawing nearer, until the woman's voice was clearly coming from the door to his left. He almost stepped through, but caught himself, grabbing the doorframe. The room beyond had no floor, and was only a pit dropping all the way back down to the water.

Across the void of the floorless room was an open door, in which Esmerelda stood, naked and filthy and thin.

He couldn't understand what she was saying. She was spitting out words between sobs, with a little laughter mixed in. Esmerelda was a fairly new arrival at the Dixie, having been traded to Doc a few months ago in exchange for a case of booze. When he'd seen her last, she'd been a shapely young thing, with sinister eyes. She'd looked like she hated everyone on Earth, and who could blame her? Now, she just looked terrified and hungry.

"Just hold on," Tony said, studying the situation. The light was nearly gone. It looked like a twenty-foot drop, maybe more, into a real mess of jagged rubble.

"Stay calm," he said. "I'll be back."

She screamed as he left the doorway.

He made it back to the boat in less than a minute. The water danced with black shadows and red flames. Night was moments away. He found his rope and ran back up the stairs.

She waited in the far doorway, quiet now, and she'd found a sheet and draped it over her body. Her eyes were wide, glistening in the gloom.

"You're real," she said.

"I try," said Tony.

She pulled the sheet tighter around her shoulders.

"What happened?" he asked.

"Soldiers came," she said. "I hid. When it got quiet, I came out. The floor was gone."

"Jesus. You've been trapped all this time?"

She looked down into the pit. He could barely understand her as she answered. "Doc said they would come for him. He said they'd kill me. I wasn't important, like him. He told me he'd made traps."

"Let's get you out of there," Tony said. "Catch."

He tossed a coil of rope. She moved to catch it, but pulled her arms back as her sheet slipped. Fortunately, the rope landed in the room, and snagged on the floor's jagged edge as it slid back.

"Okay," he said. "Are you good at knots? I need you to tie that tightly to the sturdiest thing in the room."

She slowly knelt and grabbed the rope, looking slightly dazed.

"Come on," he said. "Time's wasting. You gotta trust me."
She disappeared into the room. Tony looked at his watch.
There wasn't time for this. This wasn't how he'd planned to
spend the evening. He should go on, leave her to her own
devices. Except he hated people who thought like that, and
now was a bad time to turn into someone he hated.

"It's tied," she said, reappearing.

Tony took up the slack, then yanked on the rope, putting
his full weight on it. It felt solid from her end. He tugged the
rope to a radiator pipe in the hall and tied his end, bracing
his foot against the wall to pull it as taut as possible.

Then, without stopping to think about it, he stepped into
the room, onto the rope, which sagged beneath him. He kept
moving. Five six seven steps—and he was across, stepping
into her room. Esmerelda stood there with her mouth open.

"Let's hurry this up," Tony said with a glance at his watch.
He began to unbutton his shirt. Esmerelda backed away.

He held the shirt out to her.

"Wear this," he said. "I don't want to trip over that sheet
when I carry you back."

"C-carry me?"

"I've walked wires with both my sisters standing on my
shoulders. We'll make it."

"You're crazy," she said.

"*Jesus*," he said. "There isn't time for discussion. The Tony
Express leaves the station in one minute." He placed the
folded shirt on her shoulder, then turned around. "I won't
look."

He studied the room she'd been trapped in. It was filled
with flower pots and plastic tubs in which various green
things were growing, some with little yellow blossoms. The
room smelled like a sewer. There was a medicine cabinet on
the wall, and pipes where the tub and sink had been. The
rope was tied to the base of a shattered toilet, beside which
sat a basin of clear water. Above this was a small window,

through which he could see the night sky. He was on the wrong side of the building for the big show.

She touched his shoulder, lightly.

He turned. She wore his shirt now, which made her seem smaller, and there were tears streaming down her cheeks.

"Hey," he said. "Don't cry."

"I don't... I don't know if this is really happening. I've had... I've been having *dreams*."

"The Wolfman used to say, 'Some dreams you gotta ride.'" He pointed to his back. "Hop on."

Tentatively, she wrapped her arms around his neck. She smelled earthy, and her skin felt oily and hot against his. He lifted her. She was light, all bones and skin.

"Don't flinch," he said, and stepped onto the rope. She flinched, tightening her grip on his throat, her legs clamping around his waist. He moved cautiously, his feet listening to the messages the rope was sending. It wasn't good. Individual strands of the hemp were popping and snapping. The pipe in the hall was pulling free of its braces. Move move move *move*.

"*Alley oop!*" he cried, jumping forward. Esmerelda shrieked. He landed in the doorway and stumbled into the hall. He pried her arms off his trachea. "We made it. It's okay. It's okay."

She dropped from his back, trembling, laughing, crying.

"G-God. Oh God," she stammered. "I'm out. I'm out. I can still get to safety."

"You're as safe as you're ever going to be," he said.

"No!" she cried out. "Don't you know? Don't you know? How can you not know? There's a comet that's going to hit near here. A big one! We've only got until May 8 to get to—"

"That's today," he said. "We've got fifteen minutes."

She turned pale. She placed a hand against the wall.

Tony grabbed his stuff and headed for the stairs.

"C'mon," he said, racing up the steps two at a time.

Tony opened the door to the roof. The sky was black and silver, with a thin sliver of moon. A dozen comets streamed from the direction of the vanished sun. And to the east, a bright star, brighter than the moon, with a halo filling half the sky.

"Wow," he said.

He looked back. Esmerelda was halfway up the stairs, looking at him.

"Come on," he said. "You don't want to miss this do you? This is the kind of sky I dreamed about as a kid. A sky full of mysteries and wonders."

Esmerelda shook her head and turned, but didn't leave.

Tony shrugged. What did it matter if she didn't watch? He thought it strange, but then, everybody always thought *he* was strange, so who was he to judge? He'd planned to be alone anyway. But now that he had an audience, he was overcome with the need to talk.

"When I was ten, Mom bought me a telescope to see it," he said. "The brown star, I mean. Way out there, beyond Pluto. It wasn't much to look at. Scientists got all worked up, talking about how fast it was moving, where it had come from, where it was going, and all the damage it was doing by altering the orbits of comets. But in the telescope, it just hung there, a boring coffee-colored dot."

Tony sat down, his back against a chimney, the humidor in his lap.

"It's an exciting time to be alive, don't you think?"

She didn't answer.

Tony opened the humidor, revealing the syringe. He lifted it, and looked at the sky through the fluid-filled glass. It swirled with memories.

"You know how kids want to run away and join the circus?"

She didn't answer. He wasn't sure she could hear him.

"It works the other way around, too. My folks, my older sisters, they were the Flying Fiorentinos, Aerialists

9

Extraordinaire! Pop had big plans for me, being the first son. He had me training for the high wire while I was still in diapers."

Tony ran his finger along the old scars on his arm. "When I was about fifteen, the circus got a new snake lady, Satanica. Twice my age, but open-minded. She was a junky. Wasn't long before I was hooked, too. You can handle snakes while you're in the haze. Hell, the snakes like it. But junk and the high wire don't mix well. Pop got Satanica busted. I ran off that night to visit her in jail. Never got to see her. But I never went back to the circus."

Against the bright sky, the waves of heat from the roof shimmered and danced. Tony sighed.

"I hate my Pop. He never gave a damn about me. I was just part of his act. A *prop* or something."

He looked back at the stairs. Esmerelda sat in the doorway, her back to him. She had her face pressed against her knees, her arms locked tightly around her shins. He readied the needle. The star of the east blazed bright now, casting shadows. If his watch was right, and he'd taken a lot of care over the years to see that it was, and if the astronomers were right, and their track record through all this had been pretty good, there were nine minutes, forty seconds left.

"Three years ago, I got off the junk," he said, tying the thick rubber tube around his arm. "But I made sure I'd have one last dose. Because the best moments of my life were spent floating on junk, curled up in the arms of my snake woman. That's what I want to take with me. How 'bout you? How do you want to spend the rest of your life?"

Esmerelda spoke, her voice tense and angry. "At least you were born *before* they found the rogue star. My folks *knew*. And they brought me into the world anyway."

"Some people didn't believe," said Tony, closing his hand tightly around a wad of tissues, watching his veins rise. "And some people hoped for the best."

10

"They said *God* would take us away," she murmured. She wrapped her hair around her fists as she talked. She looked at him, her eyes flashing in sharp little slits. "I *tried*. I *can't* believe in God. How could *they*? How could *anyone*?"

"My Mom believed," said Tony, placing the needle against his skin. "Probably will to the last second. If she's even still alive."

"I *killed* mine," she said.

"What?" Tony moved the needle away from his arm.

"My parents. On my thirteenth birthday. I slit their throats as they slept. The night the comet hit the moon."

"Jesus."

"I *should* have killed *myself*."

Tony sighed, and opened his hand. "Come here."

She shook her head.

"I think you need this more than I do," he said, holding the syringe toward her.

Her eyes fixed on it. She wiped her cheeks.

"It will help you," he said. "You still have a few minutes left."

She rolled to her knees, and crawled toward him, keeping her eyes fixed on the roof.

"Here," he said, meeting her halfway, pushing up her sleeve.

He'd only used a needle on another person once before, long ago. But the skill came back easily enough. She gasped as he pushed the plunger in.

"Now breathe deep," he said.

It worked quickly, like he remembered. He rolled her over onto his lap, and she opened her eyes to the dance of the comets. He watched her as she watched the sky, for the longest time. He dared not look at his watch. If he didn't look at the watch, time would stand still. Eternities could be hidden between seconds. At last, she smiled.

"Mysteries," she whispered. "And *wonders*."

Tony lay back, lit a cigarette on the first try, and looked at the dark spaces between the comets. The black shapes curled like vast snakes. He recalled the boom-box. He'd forgotten to play the music. But things don't always go as planned. A lifetime of practice won't keep the wire from snapping. When you fall, you relax, and let the net catch you.

SECRET ORIGINS

One night, I had a dream about a man moving through a flooded city by tightrope walking on telephone wires. I woke up and jotted down "the aerialist" on a pad I kept by the side of my bed. Over the next few days, the image stuck, and I started asking the kinds of questions that helped the story form. Why did the guy know how to walk tightropes? Why was the city flooded? Bit by bit, the story came together in my head, and when I finally sat down to write it, it came out pretty much scene by scene in it's current form.

Before I wrote this story, I had a long string of unpublished stories where I had a hard time getting my heroes right. My heroes really fell into two camps. Sometimes, my hero was a competent guy who happened to be in the right place at the right time to solve the story's problem. At the other end of the spectrum, my heroes were often hapless losers, in over their heads, who'd solve the story's problems with a bit of luck and pluck.

Tony broke the mold by being both competent (as an aerialist) and a loser (as a junkie). But the biggest break from old story patterns was that he didn't really solve the story's central problem. Sure, he saved a girl stranded in a room, but fifteen minutes later she'll be dead along with him. On the surface, the story is a complete exercise in futility.

Yet, Tony never gives in to despair. In the face of inevitable death, he still manages a bit of decency and kindness. Because, sure, he only has fifteen minutes. But we're all on limited clocks. Some people reading this might be dead in fifteen days. Others might make it fifteen years, or more. In the end, there will be an end.

You're as safe as you're ever going to be.

How do you want to spend the rest of your life?

SILENT AS DUST

ଧ୍ୟଠ୍ଟାଡଠ୍ଟାଡ଼ଠ୍ଟାଡଠ୍ଟାଡଠ

The Company I Keep

I'M JUDGING a talent show in the attic of Seven Chimneys. The theatre is a maze of cardboard boxes, gray with grime. The moonlight through the round window serves as our spotlight.

First up is Dan, a deer head with five point antlers and a startled look in his glass eyes. Dan sings "Jailhouse Rock" as a blue grass ballad, accompanied by Binky, a sock monkey with a quilted banjo.

Next comes Professor Wink, an ancient teddy bear with one eye and half his fur. Professor Wink is a juggler, keeping aloft a crochet mallet, a broken lava lamp, and the ceramic manger from the Christmas decorations. When all three items are in the air, he grabs an old bowling ball and tosses it into the mix with a cool grace that earns him points.

The last act is Tulip. She's a baby doll with no left leg. Her act is to climb high into the lofty rafters of this old Victorian attic, then leap. She unpins the threadbare dishtowel someone diapered her with long ago and flips it into a parachute. She drifts toward the floor, reciting the Gettysburg Address. For her finale she lets go and dives into a white plastic bucket full of nails.

Tulip is an unusually talented baby. Also a noisy one. She lands with a clatter.

I hold my breath.

Darcy's voice from the room below: "Don't tell me you didn't hear that."

"Ish muffin," Eric mumbles, on the verge of sleep. The mattress creaks as he turns to face Darcy. "It's an old house. It has noises."

"Something's moving in the attic," Darcy says.

"Don't worry about it."

"What if it's a raccoon? They carry rabies."

The light flips on beneath me. Thin pencils of light shoot up through cracks. I creep across the rafters, light as a breath, placing my weight with practiced precision on joists I know will not creak. I hear Eric and Darcy in the hallway, near the pull-down stairs. I reach the main chimney and slither behind it, into the shaft that leads to the basement.

The springs twang as the attic steps are lowered. Light chases me as I drop into the passage and wedge myself against the bricks. I go corpse quiet. I've taught myself not to cough, fart, belch, gurgle, or sneeze. My breathing is soft and silent as cotton gauze.

Eric has clicked on the single light bulb, with its dangling chain. The bulb is coated in cobwebs; a burning smell wafts across the attic. I'm upside down in the shaft, behind five feet of brick. The yoga practice pays off. I don't feel strained. I'm free to follow the conversation as Eric pokes around, griping to Darcy, still in the hall. A bright beam flickers around the top of the shaft. He's got a flashlight to supplement the bulb. If he looks in the hole behind the chimney, my presence will be difficult to explain. As he draws closer I see the ancient red brick surrounding me. I normally make this journey in utter darkness.

"This is stupid," he says, mere feet above me. On the surface, he's talking about the search. But I hear the subtext in his voice. For two weeks they've been arguing about having a baby. Darcy's ready, Eric isn't. Every conversation is colored by this central disagreement.

"Keep looking, please," she says. My sensitive ears place her at the foot of the stairs.

"What if I find something?" Eric grumbles. The light diminishes as he turns away. "Suppose there *is* a raccoon up here. Then what?"

"Stomp on it," she says, half-joking, I think.

"It's not a spider." He sounds exasperated. He's moving around, nudging boxes with his feet. "In fact, it's not anything. It's the house. It's old. It creaks."

"I know what I heard. It wasn't the house."

"Maybe it's one of the ghosts," Eric says, moving closer to the chimney again. "I don't recall anyone dying in the attic, but it's easy to lose track."

Suddenly, there's enough light in the shaft I can see my shadow spilling down the long wall before me. This is it. "Oh my God!" he shouts, as the light jerks away. "You won't believe what I just found!"

"What?" Darcy asks, sounding scared.

"My old sock monkey! Mr. Bojangles!"

Oh, right. The monkey *was* named Bojangles. Where did I get Binky from?

"I'm coming down. An army of raccoons could hide up here. We'll call an exterminator tomorrow. Have him put out traps, if it makes you feel better."

"Okay," says Darcy.

The light clicks off.

My breath slides out of me in a long, gentle release. I loosen my grip on the brick and slink my way back down the shaft toward the cellar. I'm tempted to go back to the attic. That stupid Tulip and her noisy landing almost got me caught. I'd like to pull out her other leg. Fortunately, there's still a sane person sharing my brain that knows, deep down, I was the one who threw Tulip into the bucket. From time to time, boredom puts me in tight spots.

My name is Steven Cooper. I'm a Seven Chimneys' ghost. I've haunted the place for three years.

If haunted is the right word. Since, you know... I'm not *technically* dead.

Could Have Been a Tour Guide

IT CAN GET confusing talking about Seven Chimneys. There's the town of Seven Chimneys, a little speck on the map an hour's drive from Charlotte. The town has barely two thousand people, most living in mobile homes or old millhouses. The core of Seven Chimneys is a picturesque village that reached its prime a century ago, with a main street dominated by a dozen Victorian mansions restored by wealthy Charlotte refugees looking for the laid-back, small town life.

The grandest of these mansions is Seven Chimneys, the house, with thirteen-thousand square feet of towers, wraparound porches, and decorative woodwork. Seven Chimneys isn't a true Victorian home, since the building started shortly after the Revolutionary War. Three brothers, the Corbens, released from George Washington's army, traveled to the then nameless town and built homes close together on a single acre lot. The Corbens prospered, churning out doctors and lawyers and inventors over the coming decades. The three homesites sprawled as slave quarters were built and kitchens added on. Eventually, the houses merged together into a single Frankenstein mansion with seven chimneys..

Sometime before World War One, Franklin Corben, the railroad king, prettied up the place with a Victorian facade and extensive remodeling on the interior, adding electricity, plumbing, etc. Parts of the house in poor repair were walled off.

The hidden rooms, the dead spaces, became useful during prohibition. Behind a secret panel in the library, there's a well-stocked bar and a slate pool table that I don't think Eric knows about. He does, however, know about the wine cellar that had its entrance bricked over, with only a hidden trap door inside a pantry to give access. He was the first person to show me the coal chute at the rear of the house that leads to a furnace, and behind the furnace the narrow tunnel that leads to a bathtub in which actual bathtub gin was fermented. The place is covered in dust and spider webs now, forgotten by history. But not by me.

A Close Call

I'M DOWN IN the root cellar doing yoga with Professor Wink. I'm naked; I haven't worn clothes in two years. My pants got snagged once in the chimney and I was stuck for two days. Up above, I can hear a bustle of activity. Eric is kind enough to let the locals hold weddings at Seven Chimneys. The floor boards thud and bump with their movements. It's hard to stay tuned onto Eric and Darcy. They're talking about getting a puppy. Of course, the puppy conversation is only a substitute for the whole baby thing.

I've warmed up with the Cobbler's pose. Now I bend into the once impossible Camel as if I'm made of rubber. Professor Wink, even boneless, can't hold this pose.

"It's not like we're here most of the time," Eric argues. "A puppy needs attention. It needs time that we don't have."

"We can make time," Darcy says. "There's more to life than work. A dog will keep us focused on what's important."

"Maybe after my schedule changes, but that's no time soon. Look, the world will still be full of puppies a year from now. Let's think about it then."

Someone heavy walks overhead and I miss Darcy's response.

The artfully named "Half Lord of the Fishes" pose has me twisting my torso around to the point I can see my bony, callused butt. It's hard to believe everything I know about yoga I learned from a picture book I swiped from the library.

After a few minutes I realize I've completely lost Eric and Darcy's voices. I'll have to wait to find out if they've decided anything.

I finish my routine in the so-called Corpse pose, flat as a flounder, every muscle in my body in a state of utter release. Professor Wink is good at this one.

Then I realize someone else is here. I look toward the stairs and find a little girl standing there, staring. She's wearing a white, frilly dress; she looks like a flower girl. She's quiet, quieter than me.

We watch each other for an uncomfortably long time. I'm anticipating her scream. Any second, adults will rush down the steps.

Then, to my great relief, she silently turns and walks up the steps, vanishing back into the shadows. Probably, she'll tell people about the naked ghost in the cellar. I'll be part of the folklore. It's a living.

How I Use the Bathroom

I'M NOT ALWAYS hiding in the attic or under floorboards. Thirteen-thousand square feet, occupied by two people, means a lot of the house never gets looked at on a daily basis. Eric and Darcy have three housekeepers and a crew of landscapers, but none live onsite. Eric's an ER surgeon; he works insane shifts at Charlotte General. Darcy's a corporate acquisitions attorney and is out of town half the time. If they did get a puppy, they'd probably hire someone to watch after it.

Once the cleaning crew finishes their daily duties, I'm free to climb up from the cellar and roam around the main part of the house. I use the bathroom in the small toilet near the library. Since it's Tuesday, I shower. I stopped shaving when I moved in. A pale, wild-haired man stares back at me from the mirror. I'm thin as Ghandi. My body has become a grand collection of calluses. It's a yogi's body, the body of a holy man, limber and tough and purposeful. What that purpose may be eludes me.

They've Never Noticed My Gleaning

I'M NOT HUNGRY tonight, but I eat anyway. Eric and Darcy's refrigerator sports an assortment of half-eaten Chinese takeout.

After my meal, I creep into the library. My senses expand to cover all of Seven Chimneys. I'm tuned to Darcy's breathing as she sleeps in the master bedroom on the third floor. Eric didn't come home tonight; on his busier days, he sleeps at the hospital. I worry Eric is putting his career ahead of his marriage. Darcy deserves better. I read in the library until the predawn hours. When Darcy's breathing shifts the slight way it does every morning before her alarm goes off, I carefully shelve the books. I tiptoe to the kitchen, slip through the hidden passage in the pantry, then wiggle through the narrow gaps in the floor joists that lead to the main cellar, and the base of the big chimney.

Exactly the way I remember doing as a child.

Eric and I Go Way Back

I'VE BEEN LISTENING to Darcy and Eric argue about the damn puppy again. As usual, Eric prevails. Eric always prevails. The world has bent to his will since we were kids.

Eric and I have a bond that dates back over twenty years. Eric Corben was born to the wealth and privilege that accompanies his family name. I was born in a crumbling shotgun shack. Eric's father was an attorney and mayor of Seven Chimneys, the town, for five terms. My father was an unemployed drunk. My mother cleaned the bathrooms of Seven Chimneys, the house. I would come with her. Eric and I would play. We explored all the spooky corridors of Seven Chimneys. Or, so we thought. We never knew about the hidden bar. We found the shaft behind the chimney, but never had the courage to climb it.

Until we started school, Eric and I weren't really aware of the class differences between us. Alas, in kindergarten, cliques formed. Eric was part of the cool crowd, wearing new clothes and showing off the latest hot toys. I was the same age, several inches shorter, and went to school wearing Eric's hand-me-downs. We would have grown apart if not for a tragic coincidence. When we were both eight, Eric's mother and my father died in separate car crashes. We didn't really talk about this shared bond. But, from then on, we had each other's back.

In fairness, Eric had my back more than I had his. He'd make sure I wasn't the last kid picked for the kickball team. He let the school bullies know I was off limits. I returned the favor in high school by letting him cheat off tests and writing papers for him. Eric wasn't a dummy, by any means. If anything, public school bored him. By sixth grade, he was already weighing his college choices. He let me write his report on *Huckleberry Finn* because his attention was focused on James Joyce's *Ulysses*.

Eventually, college separated us. Eric went off to Harvard. I stayed home and attended Corben Community College. He graduated and went to medical school. I graduated and landed a job as assistant manager at a convenience store. I still had hopes and dreams, until Mom came down with breast cancer. I stayed home to care for her. She fought for six years.

In a second coincidence, Eric's father had a heart attack while attending Eric's graduation from med school. He turned blue and died surrounded by five hundred doctors. On the same day, my mother passed away in ICU, after three weeks of unconsciousness. I was holding her hand as she passed.

I went to Eric's father's funeral. He came to Mom's. I met Darcy for the first time. I learned that Eric had just accepted the position in Charlotte; he'd been planning on buying a condo, but now he and Darcy had decided it made more sense to move to Seven Chimneys and commute.

After the funerals, Eric went home to Seven Chimneys, the richest man in the county. I went back to the 1960's era silver Jetstream trailer I'd been renting after the bank foreclosed on Mom's place. I was three months behind on rent. When I pulled into the driveway, I saw the padlock. My landlord had taken the opportunity of my mother's funeral to lock me out.

My Art Museum Breathes

IN THE MIDDLE of the night, I tiptoe into the master bedroom. I like to look at Darcy while she sleeps. That sounds creepy but I'm not a pervert. What I am is a man with a decent mind who never escaped the shackles of poverty. I never traveled to Italy for a summer, like Eric has. I've never been to Paris, where they honeymooned. All I know of the great art of the world I know from books, and from the Corben art collection, which boasts a Renoir, three Wythes, and a Rembrant.

None are as lovely as Darcy. She's art, given breath. My time spent at her bedside, staring at her face, is the closest I will ever get to the Louvre. Her eyes are moving beneath her eyelids. She's dreaming. Of Eric, I wonder? Or puppies? Or ghosts?

Her breathing stills and her eyelids flutter. She turns in her sleep. Catlike, silent, I slink to the doorway as her eyes open. I'm halfway down the hall before she can possibly focus. I don't know how the rest of the world can be satisfied by art that doesn't have the possibility of looking back.

Ordinarily I Like Dogs

FRIDAY, DARCY BROUGHT home a puppy. For the last seventy hours, the dog has barked. If I'm in the attic, he barks at the ceiling. If I'm in the cellar, he barks at the floorboards. He pauses from time to time to eat or nap, but even in his sleep, he growls. Eric and Darcy are practically in tears, not knowing what to do about their insane little dog.

On Monday, Darcy skipped work to take Yippy to the vet. She tells Eric that the puppy didn't make a peep at the vet's office. The second he's returned to Seven Chimney's, he's back at the main chimney, barking, staring, as if there's some unseen stranger lurking behind the wall.

Maybe I should shower more often.

The first few days, I hoped the dog would get used to me. Now, I don't think he will.

"I told you a puppy was a bad idea," Eric says.

"You always have to be right, don't you?" Darcy snaps. I hear in her voice the beginning of the end. It would break my heart if they get divorced.

On Tuesday, they both leave for work. The housekeepers go out to lunch with the ground crew. I'm alone with the puppy.

I feel bad about what I did to shut Yippy up. He had such sad eyes. Professor Wink tries to console me with the idea that maybe I saved Eric's marriage. But maybe I haven't. I don't have a track record of getting things right.

My Life as an Action Movie

I WAS DRUNK on vodka. I was driving in the mountains in my 1982 Dodge Omni, taking curves at 60 miles an hour in a driving rain. I was coming up on the White River Gorge. I wasn't wearing my seat belt. This was three years ago.

My Omni went through the guardrail. I went through the windshield.

For a long moment I hung in the air, weightless. The rain slick hood of my car floated before me, close enough to touch. Slowly, our arcs diverged. The car dropped toward the swollen river a hundred feet below. I fell toward the tip of a tall pine, twenty feet down. I imagined I might impale myself on the tree. Instead, I tangled in the upper branches and the whole tree bowed, carrying me at decreasing speed another thirty feet until the trunk snapped, dropping me into a thick cluster of branches in a neighboring pine. I slid across the soggy needles, falling into the limbs of yet a third tree. I dropped in a painful series of snags and snaps, until I landed, crotch first, on a long bough that sagged beneath my weight, lowering me gently to the moss softened rocks by the riverside.

I stood there, stunned, as I watched the twisted scrap metal of the Omni vanish into the floodwaters. I was bleeding from a hundred scratches. My clothes were little more than tatters.

I leaned against a tree trunk, going limp, slipping down until I was flat against the soggy earth. I think I was crying; quite possibly I was laughing. As best I can remember, I said of my attempted suicide, "Son of a bitch. I can't do anything right." Maybe I'm imagining that. It seems suspiciously cool-headed, in retrospect.

Darcy's Pregnant

IT'S A CHILLY March morning when I hear Darcy break the news on the phone to her mother. I do the math; the last time they made love was on February second. Probably they fooled around on Valentine's Day, but they flew to Bermuda that weekend, so I can't be sure. There's a chance this baby will be born on Halloween. I wonder if they'll open the house for the ghost tour this year.

I don't know if Eric will be a good father. He's not the best husband. Sure, he's caring, and rich, and movie star handsome. But, he's never around. He only thinks of his career. He's not the sort of person who would give up six years of his life to care for his dying mother. I wonder if he'll tell Darcy to have an abortion.

Ghost Stories

THERE'S A PICTURE of me in the paper. I've been careless again. I was in the attic Saturday, looking out the window, watching the tourists who invade the town for the Apple Festival on Main Street. Lots of people take pictures of Seven Chimneys. I forgot to duck.

I'm clearly visible in the window. You can make out my long hair and beard, and my sunken, skeletal eyes. If you stare at the picture long enough, it's easy to reinterpret my face as the reflection of clouds on wavy glass.

The paper recounts the civil war legend of Crispus Matherton, a union soldier who'd been left for dead on the battlefield, only to stagger into town days later, disoriented, his wounds riddled with maggots. The sheriff was going to jail him, until Anne Corben intervened. Anne took the stranger home, saying even a Yankee shouldn't suffer so grievously. She bathed his wounds, dressed him in fresh linen, and fed him a hearty meal of red beans and cornbread.

That night, she smothered him with a pillow. Her husband, Colonel Randolph Corben, had been decapitated by a Yankee shell at Petersburg six months earlier.

A half dozen other ghosts keep Matherton company. Franklin Corben, the railroad guy, choked on a cocktail olive. He's been spotted by firelight in the library, reading the first edition of *Leaves of Grass* normally on display in the glass case. Sometimes, the book is missing from the case, and found on the coffee table beside the leather couch. I admit, I've moved the book a time or two.

> *I give you fair warning before you attempt me further,*
> *I am not what you supposed, but far different.*

Sometimes, in the grave-like silence of the predawn house, I wonder: Perhaps I *am* Franklin Corben, and my whole life is some odd afterlife fantasy. Perhaps I'm also Alicia Corben, the six-year-old girl who was raped and strangled in the cellar. Or maybe I'm Anthony Adams, the convict who swore revenge against Judge Harlan Corben and was blamed for Alicia's death. Adams supposedly wanders the grounds looking for his head after he was lynched by an angry mob. They dropped him too far. He dangled only a few minutes before his head came off.

There's also the possibility that I'm old Cyrus Washington, the slave who saved Anne Corben from the fire that destroyed the kitchen. He was rewarded with his freedom, but never moved away. He lived in the main house in a private room for decades until he died of carbon-monoxide poisoning from a malfunctioning gas lamp. They say he was a hundred and twelve. Supposedly, his ghost dialed the fire department in 1987 when the wiring in the back bedroom went cablooey and set the wallpaper on fire.

John Arthur Corben drowned at Pearl Harbor. His spirit found its way home when his medals were sent back to his mother. He was a gifted piano player, and sometimes, in the quiet of the night, the soft strains of Mozart are faintly heard from the grand piano. Perhaps I'm him.

Or perhaps I'm Steven Cooper, a man whose life made no impact at all upon the world. A man forgotten, unworthy of ghostly legend, a man who did nothing of significance with the breaths of air he drew. A man who lives like dust under the floor of another man's life.

A Long Walk in a Cold Rain

WHEN I WALKED back to town the night I drove off the bridge I felt invisible. The fire truck and a dozen police cars raced past me. You might have thought that they would ask the bleeding man in torn clothing what he knew about the accident. In their defense, the night was dark. After the rain stopped, the clouds hid the moon and stars. The responsible thing to do would have been to call someone and tell them not to waste time dragging the river.

I never made the phone call. Instead I walked to Seven Chimneys and pounded on the front door at five in the morning. Eric wasn't home. He'd gone to Boston to take care of some business, though I didn't know that at the time. I was soaked. I was turning blue from the bruises. I felt dreamy and numb; busting through the windshield had left the whole world with a gentle clockwise spin. When I closed my eyes, I felt weightless.

I crawled into the cellar through the window that doesn't latch. I found some Tylenol in a guest bathroom and went to sleep on a bed stuffed with goose feathers, snuggled beneath two musty old quilts. I slept for what seemed like days.

I'd been living in Eric's house for two weeks when he and Darcy moved in permanently. I thought about revealing myself, telling my story, but, at the time, it struck me as a fairly pathetic tale. What's more, I knew Eric would say something wise and caring, something perfect, the way he always does. I worried that Darcy, who I'd only met at the funerals, would look at me with pitying eyes and wonder how her new husband had managed to befriend such a loser. So, I didn't find the courage to come out of my hiding place that first day. Or the first week. By the time I'd been living side by side with them for a month, unseen, unheard, unsuspected, revealing my presence would have been awkward.

My Days Are Numbered

OF COURSE, ERIC reacts to Darcy's pregnancy perfectly. He's thrilled, you can hear it in his voice. Any doubts he might have had are gone. A white spike of jealously pins me to the attic floor. Eric lives a charmed life. He's not a parasite living off the crumbs of his childhood friend. He's married, building a career, and now he'll pass his genes to a new generation, fulfilling his highest biological purpose. The great wheel of life turns, and he's riding the wheel. I'm somewhere beneath the tread, crushed out of existence.

Only, I do exist. I have a life, of sorts. And that life is going to get complicated. Darcy's decided to leave her job. She's going to do consulting work from home. Her mother is coming down to help when she's further along. The house is never going to be empty. Darcy's always the one who hears me when I slip up. If her mother is half as sensitive, I'll never be able to relax.

They sound so happy down below. I hug Professor Wink, needing the company. I look into his dark, wise eye and silently ask where my life went wrong. *Oh, right.* The cancer mom and the deadbeat dad. The vodka and the White River Gorge. The fact I make a better ghost than person.

Suddenly, Professor Wink gets a gleam in his eye. He's thought of a fiendish plan.

The Fiendish Plan

THE KEY, OF COURSE, is to make Seven Chimneys more haunted. Gamble that Darcy won't raise her child in a gateway for spooks.

I leave the Whitman book on the table almost every night. They put a new lock on the case. It takes me three nights to pick it. I have time on my hands. For good measure, I occasionally build a roaring fire in the fireplace. I leave a half-finished martini on the coffee table.

There's an ancient Victrola in the attic, and a cobwebbed collection of warped records. The Victrola doesn't work. I take it apart. I fix a broken gear with crazy glue and a paper clip. At four in the morning, on the night of July Fourth, Eric and Darcy wake to the warbling strains of Mozart. They come upstairs to find John Arthur Corben's Army uniform unfolded beside the Victrola. I've soaked the uniform in salt water for three days. It smells like the sea.

Alicia Corben's room has barely been opened in seventy years. I normally steer clear of the place. There's an air of melancholy that hangs over the ceramic dolls lined neatly on the shelf above the small bed. When I enter the room, I catch a glimpse in the mirror. In the dim light, through the fog of dust, the whole room looks ghostly, me most of all. I'm only thirty, but my blonde hair looks colorless and gray. The face that peeks from behind my whiskers is gaunt. My body is more skeleton than muscles; my skin sags on my bones. I'm guessing I've lost fifty pounds, and I wasn't fat before.

I shake off the reflection and search Alicia's closet for a dress. I find the perfect one, all frills and pink ribbons, the color bleached with age. It's September; they've designated the room beside theirs as the baby's room. They already have a crib set up.

I leave the dress in the crib.

One of the maids finds it the next morning. Her scream is so loud, I scan the newspaper the next day for reports of earthquakes and tsunamis.

Cooler Minds Prevail

IN MY CLEVERNESS, I overlooked the possibility of third party interference. It's mid-October. By now, I hoped Eric and Darcy would be long gone, moved to a new McMansion near the hospital, a place fresh built and free of ghosts. It is not to be.

Eric is blasé about the whole affair. He's grown up with the ghosts and the legends; he's heard the creaks that sound like footsteps, the wind playing in the chimneys that sounds like human whispers. He admits to Darcy, yes, he thinks the house *is* haunted. It's been haunted for generations and the ghosts haven't hurt a soul. They've been useful, assuming Cyrus Washington really did call the fire department. Eric thinks it's kind of cool. I hate him.

Darcy's mother, Marsha, has arrived in time to take the opposite approach. She's a devout atheist; it's an article of faith that the house is ghostless. What the house isn't, she argues, is secure. The slapped together architecture of Seven Chimney's makes the alarm system installed in the seventies a joke. Marsha doesn't believe in ghosts; she does believe in pranksters. She thinks local kids are finding a way into the house and pulling these stunts. She's persuasive. Even I start thinking she might be right.

Marsha proposes a simple, obvious idea. Put security cameras throughout the house.

I am so screwed.

Fortunately, one of the maids claims to have a psychic aunt. The maid's name is Rosa; her aunt is the oddly named Tia Tomato. At least I think she said Tomato. Her accent is hard to follow. Rosa tells Marsha that sometimes the dead have unfinished business. Sometimes they don't even know they are dead, and linger on, confused and lost, growing increasingly warped and frustrated. For a reasonable fee, she'll bring Tia Tomato around to explain the situation to the ghost and/or ghosts.

Marsha fires her on the spot. All my months of hard work, down the drain, because now even Darcy is convinced that Rosa was staging the haunting in a scheme to shake them down for money. I'm pissed at Rosa, though I know she should be pissed with me. I have to remind myself Rosa really wasn't guilty of anything; she's out of a job due to my mischief.

In the aftermath, I lay low. I want the talk of installing video cameras put on the back burner. Darcy goes into labor a few weeks later. She's whisked off to Charlotte. I have the house to myself. I take a long, hot shower. For the first time in years, I shave. I cut my hair, cropping it short to the scalp. I gather up all my trimmings in a plastic grocery bag. There's a lot of me to throw away.

In the mirror, I see the man I used to be. Do I see the man I might be again?

Crib Death

THE BABY'S BEEN HOME for two weeks. It cries a lot; it's almost as bad as the puppy. I get some relief when they take it out to the car and drive around the neighborhood. Apparently, the baby sleeps like a baby when they drive.

In fairness, it dozes off at other times as well. Starting at two in the morning, the baby can reliably be counted on to slumber for at least a few hours. During this time, Eric, Darcy, and Marsha sleep like corpses.

It's three in the morning on a Saturday. I'm at the foot of the crib, staring at the infant. They've named him Franklin. Franky, he'll be called. As he grows, he's going to explore every inch of this house. He's going take a flashlight and poke around the cellars. He'll spend hours in the attic, clawing through two centuries of clutter. He'll play with Tulip and Professor Wink and Bojangles.

I'm afraid of Franky.

Kids know all the best hiding places. Kids imagine their house is full of hidden panels and trap doors and secret passages—and this particular kid will be right. One day, he's going to find me.

Approximately one baby in a thousand dies from Sudden Infant Death Syndrome. They pass away quietly in their sleep for no reason at all. This is today, with modern medicine. Think about this house, dating back to Colonial times, when babies had the mortality rate of goldfish. I don't know of actual numbers, but I'm guessing a dozen babies have died in Seven Chimneys. A hundred, maybe.

It's a dark thing to stand beside a crib contemplating a hundred dead babies.

I reach out my hand, holding it inches over Franky's pink little face.

I linger a moment, unable to move closer, as if an invisible hand has caught my wrist and holds it with supernatural strength.

I can't swallow. My mouth is dry.

I can't do it. A puppy is one thing. If I do this, though, I'll cross a line. I'll no longer be a ghost.

I'll be a monster.

I release my breath, silent as dust.

Franky really is a cute baby.

No longer blocked by the moral barrier, I lower my hand to stroke his pink, plump cheek.

Again, my fingers stop short. It's not my imagination. Something is holding my wrist.

"I'm not going to hurt him," I mumble, saying it half to myself, half to the unseen thing gripping my arm.

I watch as dust swirls in the dim moonlight, and a second shadow appears on the wall beside my own. Bony old fingers the color of coffee materialize on my wrist. My eyes follow the arm upward, to find a skeletal old man, his face dark beneath a halo of white hair. His expression is stern; his eyes are thin slits.

"Cyrus?" I ask.

He says nothing.

"I won't hurt him," I say.

Then, a third shadow, and a fourth. A soldier stands beside me, gray and grainy as old film. He's soaked. Water pours from his clothes, chilling my bare feet.

Beside the soldier, a little girl with sad eyes shakes her head slowly. She looks familiar; was she the girl in the cellar? She's little more than mist; I can see right through her to the mirror on the back of the door.

Then I realize I'm seeing only a sweater over a chair in the mirror; in the moonlight, it drapes like a girl's dress. My feet are cold — it's an October night in a house with hardwoods like ice — but they're dry. The soldier was nothing more than the shadow of a tree.

And Cyrus? Cyrus is still standing there, oak solid. He whispers, in a voice of rustling leaves: "We're watching you, boy."

He vanishes as the headlights of a passing car sweep across the room.

I rub my wrist. My whole arm is numb. I decide that Franklin's chubby little cheeks are best left uncaressed.

After a quick trip to the attic, I go to the laundry room and steal some clothes. Eric's jeans invoke a certain sense of deja vu; it's not the first time I've worn his used pants. His old tennis shoes are too big for me; I compensate with two pairs of socks.

Then, I'm out the door, into the open sky. Leaves crunch beneath my feet as I walk across the lawn. On the front porch, a line of Jack-o-lanterns grin, a few still faintly aglow with the last flickers of their candles. I reach the end of the sidewalk and glance back at Seven Chimneys, before crossing the road and taking my return step into the wider world.

Beneath my arm, I cradle Professor Wink.

He's going to miss the place.

Me, not so much. Even with thirteen-thousand square feet, some places are just too crowded.

SECRET ORIGINS

I used to live in Petersburg, Virginia. The city and the surrounding towns had played an important role in the Civil War. Everywhere you looked, there were historical markers documenting some event that had happened nearby.

I had a friend who lived in a house that dated from before the Civil War. His home had actually been used as a hospital during the war, and he had a photograph of General Grant standing on his front porch. At least, it might have been Grant. Photography was a bit blurry back then.

My friend contended that his house was haunted. He said that, one day, he'd been watching TV when he noticed a shadow in the hall. He'd gotten up and watched a woman dressed like a Civil War era nurse walk up the steps toward the upstairs bedrooms. He was 100% positive he'd seen a ghost.

I told him that I was willing to grant he'd seen a woman in a period clothing in his

house. But, Civil War tourism was big
business in the area. Actors in uniforms
weren't a rare sight. Maybe someone playing
a Civil War nurse had snuck into his house
to check it out, not knowing anyone was
home? Maybe she mistook it for a public
building, since there was a historical
marker in front of it?

He thought this was the most absurd idea
he'd ever heard. The spirit of a dead woman,
that he could believe. A flesh and blood
woman inside his house without his
permission? Completely implausible.

Our discussion about living people haunting
houses happened probably a good fifteen
years before I wrote "Silent as Dust."
Sometimes, it takes a while for an idea to
fully germinate.

FINAL FLIGHT OF THE BLUE BEE
ଌଈଔ୲ଌଵ୲ଌଵ୲ଌଵ୲ଌଵ୲ଌଵ୲ଌଈ

WHEN THE OLD MAN came out of the bathroom wearing the faded costume, Honey placed her hand over her mouth to stifle a giggle. The black and yellow fabric over his round stomach was stretched skin-tight, revealing several inches of white, hairy flesh between his belly button and metallic gold underwear. The sleeves and leggings of the costume sagged, as if once filled by muscles that had vanished long ago. In the center of his chest was an appliqué bee, the silver foil wings crinkled and ripped. He looked away from her, studying himself in the mirror. She wondered how he saw at all in the black mask that concealed the upper half of his face, the eyes hidden by thick, gold, faceted lenses.

"A little early for Halloween, isn't it?" Honey said.

"Yes," he said, frowning.

Recognizing she'd offended him, Honey assumed her best poker face.

"So," she said. "You're a bee."

"Yes," he said.

"You, uh...," she paused, biting her lip. He showed you the money, she thought. Don't blow this. "You wanna talk about it?"

"*Buzzzzzzzz*," he said.

35

THEY'D LET MICK PAYTON out of prison with a new suit and $147 in his pocket. He'd declined the halfway house's offer to send a car to pick him up. He walked out the gate and didn't look back. It was twelve miles to the small town of Starksville. He needed the fresh air, the sunshine. Bees danced in the flowering fields as he walked past.

By that evening he'd blown half the money, starting with a T-bone dinner. The meal cost an outrageous $12. Back in 1964, you could eat out for a week on $12. Once he'd finished, he'd walked to a hardware store and spent a breath-taking $15 on an axe. Finally, the bus ticket to Collinsville, New Jersey, set him back $50. By now, he was braced for the extra zeroes that followed the prices. He tried to shrug it off. Once he reached Collinsville and the old farm, money wouldn't matter.

"YOU HAVEN'T HEARD of the Blue Bee?" the old man asked.

"Blue?" Honey asked, studying his costume, which didn't have a stitch of blue.

"He was my mentor," he said. "I was his partner, Stinger."

"Okay," she said. "Stinger."

"What's your name?" he asked.

"Honey," she said, instantly regretting it. She'd spent the better part of the week practicing the name Xanadu and now she'd blown it.

"That's not your real name," Stinger said.

And yet, it was. It was her childhood nickname, the name her father called her, and the fact that she would now be "performing" under the name bothered her. It also bothered her that the one honest thing about her that had slipped out of her mouth tonight was being treated as a lie.

"I suppose Stinger's on your birth certificate?" she said.

"You don't understand." The old man lowered his head, staring at his shimmering gold booties. "Our secret identities, they were important to our mission. Vital.

Without them, our enemies could have... could have attacked our loved ones. Those of us who had loved ones."

The seriousness of his voice, the sad sincerity — Honey suddenly understood that this wasn't a joke. She raised her hand to cover her mouth, but it was too late. The laughter exploded from her.

THE FAMILY FARM looked like it hadn't been visited since 1964. Thickets of brush covered the fields where the cows once grazed. The old barn leaned at a 15 degree tilt, and most of the roof had fallen in. Out back, the once white hive boxes were black with mildew, half rotted. Only the tiny, three-room farmhouse stood unchanged.

Mick used the axe to break the door open. Inside, the kitchen was exactly as he'd left it when his grandmother died. But one thing was new — the hellish ceaseless vibration that trembled the walls.

He pulled down the door to the attic to discover that the entire space had been filled with a maze of honeycomb. The attic was now a single, giant hive.

"How perfect," Mick said. "*Buzz. Buzzzz. Buzzzzzzzzzz.*"

In response, a swarm of bees coalesced, forming a living carpet on the stairs. Slowly, gracefully, the locked suitcase appeared at the top of the stairs, gliding down the carpet of bees to come to rest at Mick's feet.

He unlocked the latches with trembling hands, then took a deep breath before opening it.

The trunk was half full of twenty dollar bills. He could buy all the T-bones he wanted now. Sitting neatly atop the money was his spare costume, folded smoothly, the gold and silver gleaming like treasure. And atop this, his back-up Sting-gun, plus a dozen vials of pheromone and venom.

He picked up the vials and studied the cloudy fluid, swirling in the dying light.

All the tools he'd need to enforce payment of the old debt.

STINGER SAT on the edge of the bed. He shook his head. "Laughed at by a whore," he said, his shoulders sagging. "The future is a rough place."

Honey wiped the tears from her face, smudging her fingers with mascara. His use of the word "whore" sobered her. So blunt—and so accurate. What did it matter that this was her first time? What did it matter that she'd been in New York for six months without a job and all of her money was gone and she was 48 hours away from eviction? Nothing erased the fact that she'd made the decision to rent her body for money. She could have been approached by any number of horrible creeps. This old man was strange, but he didn't seem dangerous. She needed to be more professional.

"About the costume," she said. "I'm cool with it. Whatever floats your boat."

"This isn't some sexual thing," Stinger said. "Back then, there were whispers, of course. You'd have to be blind not to see I was a lot younger than Blue Bee. He was thirty-five, I was twenty, but looked younger. I remember when our archenemy the Hatchet called Blue Bee a pedophile. That really set Blue Bee off. I thought he was going to cripple the Hatchet. Beat him for ten minutes. There wasn't a tooth left in that bastard's mouth afterwards."

"You were, uh, some kind of superhero? A real one?"

"Yes! My God, 40 years isn't that long. You remember the Beatles don't you? You remember Ed Sullivan, and JFK, and Vietnam?"

"I've heard of them, sure."

"But not of Blue Bee and Stinger?"

"Sorry."

Stinger stared into the mirror. Honey got on her knees behind him and rubbed his shoulders.

"We saved the world," he said. "And the world's forgotten."

THEY'D REACHED MR. MENTAL before the police. They were always a step ahead of the police.

Mr. Mental stared the Blue Bee down, a touch of madness in his eyes, as he announced:

"I control the H-bombs. All of them." He tapped his silver helmet. "I know the launch codes. I have the detonators primed. A single thought, and I trigger Armageddon."

"You fiend," Blue Bee said, straining against the bars of the cage that had dropped from the ceiling. Blue Bee looked terrific in his skin-tight navy costume. He had a Charles Atlas build, and when he was angry his eyes took on this fiery, determined cast that made Mick feel that he was in the presence of a true man, a hero.

And that day, climbing through the window behind Mr. Mental, listening to him brag about the bombs, Mick stood in the presence of a true villain. He could have tried something clever. A tap on the shoulder, a quick quip, a punch to the jaw. He could have somersaulted across the room with acrobatic grace and kicked open the bars of Blue Bee's cage. He could have commanded that bees swarm Mr. Mental, and told him to stay still or get the stinging of his life.

But there were all those bombs to think about. Literally, the fate of the world might be decided by what he did next.

So Mick silently placed his Sting-gun about an inch from Mr. Mental's spine, set the dial to ten, and shot him with a needle that pumped in a quart of venom. Mr. Mental slumped to the floor in severe anaphylactic shock. He was dead by the time Mick unlocked Blue Bee's cage.

The police kicked open the door, led by the Commissioner, who hated vigilantes.

"Our work here's done. We'd best buzz off," Blue Bee said, leaping from the window to grab the ladder dangling from the waiting Bee-Wing.

"Yeah, hate to be a drag on your little sting operation," Mick said, perching in the window, glancing back with a white-toothed grin.

The Commissioner shot him in the shoulder. Mick toppled from the window, his hand stretched out, spots dancing before his eyes, when a second bullet caught him in the thigh. Blue Bee reached for him. The tips of his gloved fingers brushed Mick's wrist.

Then Mick fell, nine stories, his life spared by a bounce from the hotel awning, and a crash landing through the roof of the Commissioner's car.

"SO," SAID HONEY. "We gonna do something, or what?"

"Yeah," said Stinger, sagging on the edge of the bed, lost in thought. "Probably."

"You want to... you want to leave the mask on?"

"Yes," he said.

She brought her lips near his ears and said, the way she'd practiced, "Just tell me what you want, baby."

Stinger chuckled, then sighed. "What I want? Justice."

Honey tensed slightly. "I, um, don't think that's on the menu. How about...?" She leaned in close and whispered a suggestion she didn't quite have the guts to say out loud.

Stinger shook his head. "I don't think so."

"Then how about—"

He cut her short by saying, "The rumors about us, they were right. We were, well, I believe the current popular term is gay. Blue Bee was my lover. My God, he was something. He had a body like a Greek statue."

"Oh," Honey said, pulling back, leaning against the headboard. "Then why am I here?"

"Because I still have needs."

"Okay, baby, okay," she said. Maybe she could still get some money out of him. "Just tell me what you need."

"A hostage," Stinger said.

THREE WEEKS IN the hospital and Robert didn't come to see him once. Not a terrible shock, he supposed. Mick had been unconscious when they pulled off his mask. He was gratified to learn that he was listed on the hospital charts as John Doe. They didn't recognize him. Why should they? He had no life outside of being Stinger, and no relatives now that his grandmother had died. Publishing his photo in the paper didn't turn up any leads. They'd fingerprinted him, but he'd never had any real trouble with the law. If millionaire physician Robert E. Eggers were to suddenly drop in to visit the John Doe handcuffed to the bed, it wouldn't take a terribly clever person to connect the dots.

The police had quite a case against him. The murder weapon had his prints on it. He'd been caught fleeing the scene of the crime. The final blow — after he'd healed enough to eat solid food again, he'd been taken down to the police station and interrogated under bright lights for five hours. The police hadn't been shy about banging on his casts, or landing punches on areas of his body already bruised and broken. He'd finally admitted to shooting Mr. Mental. The guy's real name turned out to be Paul Carpenski, who'd made his living as a hypnotist on the Jersey Shore before becoming a bank robber.

"He was going to detonate the world's nuclear arsenal with his electro-helmet," Mick protested. "I'm a hero, not a criminal."

The commissioner tossed the helmet onto the table before him.

"This is an army helmet wrapped in tin foil, kid," the Commissioner said. "Now, you going to tell us your name, or not? After they sweep your ashes out of the electric chair, wouldn't you like your headstone to say something other than John Doe?"

Despite the beatings, the threats, the tricks and promises of a bargain, Mick never broke. He never told them his name, or betrayed the Blue Bee. He claimed partial amnesia after his nine-story fall, claimed he couldn't remember who he had been before that final confrontation, and eventually they'd given up. Perhaps they believed him. Certainly, his boyish good looks, his stoic air, and his insistence that he'd done the world a favor by killing Mr. Mental, swayed the jurors. They found him not guilty of first degree murder. But manslaughter, assault with a deadly weapon, breaking and entering, resisting arrest, all brought in guilty verdicts. At twenty, Stinger, a.k.a. John Doe, secretly Mick Payton, found himself in jail for 40 years to life.

If he'd ever ratted out the Blue Bee, he could have cut his sentence in half.

THE WORD DIDN'T quite register with Honey. It seemed to be from some foreign language, nonsense noises strung together.

"Hostage?" she asked.

Stinger turned toward her and held up a Dixie cup full of yellow fluid. She couldn't tell what it was. Then, without warning, he threw it on her.

"What the hell are you doing?" she yelled. She sniffed the drops of the yellow fluid that trembled in the light hairs of her arm. It didn't smell like urine. It smelled nice, actually, like daffodils. Still, that was no excuse.

Outside the hotel window, there was a noise like a train passing. The mirror on the wall began to tremble and dance.

Stinger rose from the bed and pulled open the curtains. It was dark out, even the city lights were blotted, hidden behind a moving curtain of particles that pattered against the window like angry rain. Stinger was humming a constant "*zzzzzz*" noise through clenched teeth.

Then, with a kung-fu shout, Stinger thrust his hand forward in a sharp punch. The window shattered. Honey shrieked as a cloud of bees swarmed in, engulfing her in a black and gold tornado.

"Don't struggle," Stinger said. "You'll make the bees nervous."

"AAAAAAAA!" Honey cried. "Oh God! Oh God! Please! Don't!"

Stinger grabbed her arm and dragged her from the bed. She closed her eyes as bees climbed over her face, their tiny feet tickling her eyelids, their flickering wings teasing her nostrils. She screamed, her mouth wide, and bees crawled on her tongue, and on the inside of her cheeks. Her whole body grew encased by the vibrating, crawling blanket. In utter terror, she fell silent and still, not even breathing. Slowly, the bees crawled from the inside of her mouth.

"Bees are interesting creatures, don't you think?" Stinger's voice sounded far away, nearly lost under the drone of the swarm. "Quite orderly — one might even say civilized. They can communicate by dancing. Can you imagine what the world might be like if mankind relied on dance to communicate with one another? It's their beautiful world. It's not our world. They swim in an atmosphere of pheromones. Their music is the rumble of ultrasound. Their skies glimmer in ultraviolet. It's like a parallel universe, in the same space as ours, where flowers have patterns and shapes invisible to us. For a bee, the air is crisscrossed by highways of scent, which stand out as clear and well marked as our modern roads. And your screams — the vibrations are heard by their entire body. Have you ever felt the subway rumble underneath your feet without actually being aware of the noise? Bees hear everything this way."

Honey could hold her breath no longer. She sucked in air through clenched teeth. Then, barely parting her lips, she whispered, "Please let me go."

"I'm impressed that you haven't fainted," said Stinger. "Back in 1964, girls were always fainting. You future women are made of stern stuff."

"This is crazy," she sobbed.

"Honey," he said. "I'm dressed like a damn bee. We can discuss crazy if you really want."

"Please, please, please, get them off." She felt like the bees on her eyes were drinking up her tears. By some miracle, it didn't feel like any had stung her. "Please. I'm allergic to bees."

"Ironically," said Stinger, "so was I."

MICK HAD BEEN a sickly youth. He was allergic to everything. He'd been beaten up regularly at school, until his grandmother had paid for judo lessons when he was fifteen. Suddenly, his small, almost girlish frame was no longer an invitation for beatings. In the span of a year, he'd gotten his black belt, and placed nine bullies flat on their backs, out cold. Alas, this only resulted in multiple suspensions and eventually he'd been kicked out of school.

He'd helped his grandmother on the farm. Unfortunately, she'd kept bee-hives—they'd been at the farm for half a century, and the honey provided a steady income. But Mick had been hospitalized three times in the last year, and the cost of treating him exceeded the income the honey brought in. One day there was an article in the paper about a physician, Dr. Robert E. Eggers, who'd developed a radical new allergy treatment. His grandmother had used the last of her savings to see that Mick became one of Dr. Eggers' patients.

What a whirlwind of events—the experimental therapy, a mix of venom and radiation, had nearly killed Mick. In desperation, Robert had taken the comatose teen to the one place on the planet that had the equipment needed to save him—the Bee Hive, the Blue Bee's cavernous secret headquarters.

Mick came out of his coma stronger than ever, his muscles swelling and growing as he followed Robert's training advice and secret pollen-based vitamin therapy. To his amazement, Mick possessed new senses, could smell things he hadn't smelled before, and see in spectrums of light that had once been hidden. With his newly heightened sense of smell, it didn't take long for him to identify Robert as the Blue Bee. Robert responded by presenting him with a costume and a Sting Gun on his eighteenth birthday. The amazing team of Blue Bee and Stinger was born.

And in secret, far from the public eye, the private team of Mick and Robert found love.

AS A CHILD, Honey's family had attended a church with a fire-and-brimstone pastor. Week after week, her young mind had been filled with dread of the torments of Hell. She'd endured restless, nightmare-plagued nights for years.

None of her worst nightmares rivaled this.

She was blind. The touch of bees on her eyelids glued her eyes shut with a force her strongest desires for light could never overcome. A mask of bees crawled over her face, sparing only a small circle around her nose. The bees on her clenched lips squelched her yearning need to scream or beg for mercy. The thought of bees swarming into her again left her throat Sahara dry, her tongue glued to the roof of her mouth. She could hear only the drone of a million wings, the sound traveling through her bones, as the bodies of bees burrowed into her ears.

She no longer had any concept of up or down. The bees moved her, supporting her weight, carrying her along a lumpy, lurching carpet. The mass of the bees was unreal, like a thousand heavy woolen quilts piled upon her, entombing her. The heat boiled copious, fevered sweat from her entire body. She could feel—or perhaps imagine—a million tiny tongues licking at her moist skin.

The mass of bees smelled vaguely of clover, yeast, and urine.

Where were they taking her? Time was impossible to gage. Occasionally, she would hear distant, muffled noises. A gun shot? Stinger shouting? The dinging of elevator bells?

She may as well have been trapped in a barrel of cement for all the sense she could make of what was happening.

At last, after what might have been hours, the bees retreated from her ears. Cool air rushed against them, a whistling of wind.

"He'll love this," Stinger said.

The chill touch of the wind found her lips. The bees there had left.

"Oh, God," Honey said, sucking in air. "Oh God oh God oh God."

"From your profession, I wouldn't have guessed you to be religious," Stinger said.

"Please," she said. "Please don't kill me."

"I can't make any promises," he said.

"Please. Not like this. Not dressed in lingerie, wearing this make-up. Oh God, what will my parents think?"

"One advantage of being an orphan," said Stinger. "I never had any awkward conversations. If I'd had folks, they probably wouldn't have been thrilled by my career choice. I'm sure your folks aren't happy."

"M-my real name isn't Honey," she said. She remembered hearing in movies that it's important to remind kidnappers that you were a real person. So, as surreal as it seemed to make conversation buried under a mound of bees, she continued: "My real name's Barbara. I'm from Dayton, Ohio. I came here to be an actress and only do this to pay rent. I have a mother, a father, two sisters—they don't know I'm a hooker. I don't want to die and have them find out what I've been up to on the evening news. Please, please, let me go."

"If you could see where you are, you'd be more careful with your words," Stinger said.

"You said you were a hero! A superhero! Why are you doing this? Why?"

"Because heroes work for justice, right? Wrong. The Blue Bee, he had forty years. He could have broken me out of jail at any time. He ignored me. I did 40 years hard time before making parole. The Blue Bee, he had money. Impossible, unimaginable wealth. He could have pulled strings. He could have hired attorneys. He was a master of disguise—he had alternate identities set up. He could have helped me, but he didn't."

"I'm sorry," Honey said.

"He's vanished, you know. The Blue Bee hasn't seen action in 40 years. I watch the papers."

"He might be dead," Honey said. "How do you know he'll come here? Even if he's alive, he might be in a home by now. He'd be in his seventies."

"He's alive," said Stinger. "His secret identity—the obituary appeared years ago. But it had a code phrase in it, to let me know he'd assumed one of his cover identities. I just don't know which one."

"Where... where are we? It feels like I've been carried around a lot? It sounds like were up high some place? Oh God. They're crawling on my eyes. Please, please take them off my face at least. Please."

Stinger sighed. He hummed a little noise, deep in his throat, and the bees crawled away from her face and neck.

She opened her eyes and looked down, to police lights flashing a hundred impossible stories away. She was hanging over open space, supported by a bridge of bees.

The scream long suppressed tore from her lips, echoing in the canyons of the city below.

"We're on top of the Empire State Building, my little Fay Wray," Stinger said. "It's perfect. All the cops in the city are below us. My swarms have emptied the entire building. My bees are instructed to clog the air intakes of helicopters. No one's getting up here without a Bee Wing."

Honey screamed again, until every last spoonful of air was gone. Then she filled her lungs and screamed some more.

"Yeah," said Stinger. "That's the stuff. I bet they hear that down there. I wonder if they can get a close-up of your face? What they can do with TV cameras these days—amazing. I was a real science fiction fan back in 1964. This world astounds me. My wildest dreams couldn't top it. Look at all those lights!"

Honey fought to get control of her panic and her vertigo. Suddenly it wasn't screams coming from her lips, but vomit. She hadn't had any food all day, so only long strings of drooling acid shot from her lips. She spat, trying to clear the bitter taste from her mouth.

She felt completely empty, hollow as a dry gourd. If the bees were to drop her now, she wouldn't mind. She would float to earth on the winds, weightless as a leaf.

"All screamed out?" Stinger asked. "That's okay. I'm sure they've got plenty of footage by now."

Honey felt lighted headed and dreamy. Her situation assumed a certain nightmarish logic. "What if... what if he doesn't come by morning? Are you going to let me go? You can't wait here forever."

"Honey," he said. "I waited forty years. Blue Bee might be in Hawaii, for all I know. I'm prepared to give him time. We've got a lot of media below. With luck, it won't take too long for him to hear about this."

"Do they even know I'm up here? I was covered by bees."

"Of course. Right now, I've created a ten-foot grid on the street below. It's like a blackboard. My bees land in it and form messages. I've told them I have a hostage. I've told them not to try anything stupid. And I've told them I want the Blue Bee."

"W-won't the bees get tired? What if they drop me? You'll go back to prison."

"I'm never going back inside," said Stinger. "I either escape this cleanly or die a bloody, violent death. Don't worry about the bees getting tired. I coated you with enough pheromone to attract every bee in the state. Pound for pound, bees are much stronger than people. You've got, oh, maybe three, four tons of bees working to keep you from going plop prematurely."

"Prematurely? You don't need to kill me at all. They know I'm up here. Put me someplace safe now. Please."

"Honey, you just don't get it. There's a rhythm to these things, a ritual. If only you could have seen the Blue Bee at his peak, you'd understand. The way he'd swoop in, graceful and acrobatic, snatching the damsel in distress away from the teeth of danger at the last possible second... it was impossible not to love him, in these moments. He made me feel like he was something more than human." Stinger closed his eyes and smiled.

"You're putting me in danger so your ex-boyfriend can save me?"

"You... or me, possibly. If there's anyone in the world who can find a way out of this for me, it's him. My life has become a sort of horrible trap from which I can't see any graceful escape. But the Blue Bee... he always escaped in the end. He came out on top no matter what. He'd said there was no problem in the world that couldn't be solved by finding the right bad guy to sock in the jaw."

"Don't you see that you're the bad guy? If he's even still alive, if he's not in a wheel chair somewhere, you're the bad guy he's going to sock. Don't you want to be one of the good guys?"

"I've spent forty years in prison," Stinger said, his voice hard and cold. "I was a young man with a pretty face, half-crippled from my injuries. You can't imagine what I endured. I had plenty of time, more than enough time, to stop feeling like a hero, and see myself for what I really am. You learn a lot of things about yourself inside."

"You can't... you can't let these things haunt you," said Honey.

"That's the damn point of prison!" Stinger said, waving his Sting-gun for emphasis. "The whole system is designed to haunt you. Some folks, maybe, have it easy. Maybe they're in for a crime they didn't commit. But you know, it's an awful, awful thing to be in for a crime you're guilty of. I did kill Mr. Mental. I don't know that I could call him innocent, but maybe he was harmless. He was play acting in a game he didn't understand. And so was I. I was a man-boy caught up in a fantasy I confused with reality, playing dress-up, living like every damn day was Halloween. I had my God-given mission to save this world from crazy guys in funny hats. What a little self-righteous prick I was."

Honey blinked away tears. She could tell from the tone of Stinger's voice he would never, ever, let her leave the top of the building alive.

Her tears made the world wavy. All the city lights were surrounded by halos. From the corner of her eye, a shimmering, dark shape raced toward her with breathtaking speed.

Though she'd never seen it before, she knew instantly: It was the Bee-Wing. It was a kind of dark-blue glider with a pair of silver wings buzzing at the rear. A long, silver rope hung from the glider, ending in a bar, from which hung a big, beefy man in a navy blue suit. He wore a domino mask and a bowler with a golden BB affixed to it. The Bee-Wing flashed by, blowing her hair, and the masked man extended his arm as he sliced through the air toward her. With a horrible, rib-crushing impact, his shoulder caught her in the belly, folding her in two, draping her over him, as they hurtled upward.

"Oh no you don't!" Stinger yelled.

As spots danced before her eyes, Honey could barely make out a silver lasso flashing upward, snaring the Blue Bee's ankle. Suddenly, their upward flight jerked to a halt as the Bee-Wing ripped away. They cut a rapid arc through space, back over the observation deck. Blue Bee grabbed her, yanking her to his chest, curling up to shield her as they smacked onto the concrete deck at sixty miles an hour. She was flung away on the impact, skidding across the concrete, crashing into the steel safety bars at the edge. Dazed, she sat up, propping herself against the bars. She looked down at her naked legs and arms. She looked like she'd been sliding across a cheese grater. Worse, her lingerie was ripped, nearly gone, and dozens of bees covered her belly, struggling for freedom, their stingers impaled in her milky skin.

A dozen feet away, the Blue Bee rolled over to his back. His blue suit was torn, revealing a steel exoskeleton and padding over thin limbs. He coughed, sending a spray of blood into the air. Stinger walked toward him, swapping out his Sting-gun for a gleaming black pistol.

"Mick," the Blue Bee gasped.

"Don't you...," Stinger said, his voice choking. "Don't you dare. You son-of-a-bitch."

"Mick, we —"

"Shut up!" Stinger took aim.

Then, the Bee-Wing, its autopilot set to return to Blue Bee, swooped in with an angry drone and caught Stinger in the throat, lifting him, throwing him backward, right over the edge of the building. Suddenly the bees went crazy, swarming down in a tornado formation.

With a whir of gears, the Blue Bee sprung to his feet and rushed toward Honey. From the inner folds of his jacket, he pulled out a glass bottle with a spray top and began soaking Honey with the blue fluid inside.

"Don't panic, Miss," he said. "I see he's misted you with an attractant. This will negate it. No bee will want to come within ten feet of you with this pheromone."

"I've been stung!" Honey said. "Oh god! I'm allergic! I can feel my throat closing! I'm going to die!"

"Calm down," the Blue Bee said. He sat the bottle of repulse-pheromones next to her, then reached into his jacket again, producing a syringe and a flashlight. "I'm a doctor."

He jammed the syringe into her thigh and pushed the plunger. Then he clicked on the flashlight. Instantly, in the middle of the night, Honey developed a sunburn.

"UV radiation activates my special anti-venom," the Blue Bee said, his voice calm and reassuring despite the blood dripping from his mouth. She could see now how thin and frail he truly was. His skin was as wrinkled and thin as crumpled newspaper, stained with brown and blue ink. "This won't merely save you from your present stings. It's a permanent cure. It would have made me a thousand times richer than I already was if the government had ever learned to appreciate the side-effects."

"Can we... can we talk about this at an emergency room?" she asked. "Not that I don't trust you."

"Let me buzz the Bee-Wing." The Blue Bee rose, walking away a dozen yards, leaning over the rail as he let out a whistle and raised his hand.

He stood there, silently, hand outstretched for several long seconds. He cleared his throat and said, "It wasn't my fault."

"What?" Honey asked.

"Leaving Stinger in prison. It was... I mean...," he lowered his hand, wiping the blood from his chin. "I was married, back then. After the Mr. Mental fiasco, my wife... she had me committed. I had electroshock therapy. A lot of what went on... my old life... it's lost forever."

"I'm sorry," Honey said.

"Robert!"

It was Stinger's shout, barely audible above the horrid, rising whirr of bees. Suddenly, Stinger was lifted above the edge of the deck, standing atop a dense column of gold and black insects.

"You aren't going anywhere, Robert!" Stinger yelled. "Forty years of hate I owe you! Forty years of degradation and abuse and betrayal! Forty years!"

Stinger motioned, waving his hands forward, and twin fists of bees slammed into the Blue Bee's midsection. The old man fell to his knees. In seconds, the swarms coalesced around the old man's head, hiding his face. The bees began to shoot in from the sky like tiny, angry bullets, until his head was encased in a living globe the size of a pumpkin, and the Blue Bee toppled over. His muffled screams could barely be heard over the buzzing.

"I know you're immune to the stings," said Stinger. "So I'm simply going to drown you. I'm going to fill your lungs and throat and mouth and nose. It's going to be slow. It's going to be painful. Just like those forty years!"

Honey looked down at the bottle of pheromone, still half full. It must work, since the bees weren't coming anywhere near her. Despite the jagged pain in her ribs, she pulled herself up against the iron rails. She unscrewed the bottle cap as she staggered toward the Blue Bee. But her plan to pour the stuff over him proved unnecessary. As she approached, the bees engulfing him seemed pushed away by an invisible hand. By the time she reached him, his face was hairy with black stingers, but, save for the bees that struggled to escape his lips, the last bees had fled.

"I should have dropped you," Stinger said.

"Yeah," said Honey. "Probably."

She hurled the bottle with a strength that shocked her, striking Stinger dead center of the appliqué bee on his torso.

The bees beneath his feet boiled away. Stinger fell from the sky like a stone. He shouted something, perhaps some curse, or defiant quip, or an urgent final message to the man who'd shaped his life—but the howl of the swarm covered his words.

"Are you all right?" Honey asked, her strength ebbing as she lowered herself beside the Blue Bee.

"Not this time," Blue Bee said, gasping for breath, bees still crawling from his lips. He spat, then spat again, bloody bees flying. "Venom won't get me. But they've stung me from inside. Lungs feel full of needles. Not the sort of injury this old body's going to shake off. What a way to go."

Honey was dizzy, fighting to stay conscious. She couldn't tell if those last words were a curse, or an exultation.

Darkness ate away the edges of her vision as the doors to the roof opened and the NYPD's finest poured onto the scene.

HONEY WOKE IN the hospital three days later, feeling stronger than she'd ever felt in her life. Her parents were at her bedside—they told her she'd been in a coma, and that it was a miracle, simply a miracle that she was alive.

And perhaps it was. Something about the events of that night had transformed her. The person she had once been — the lost, desperate girl with no money and no hopes, had passed away. She felt born again. The air felt fresher, the world looked brighter, her arms and legs felt full of iron springs, as if she could leap across rooftops. She could feel the rumble of machinery far away in the hidden depths of the hospital, could hear the electricity humming in the wires of her room. And when the nurse brought in flowers, she could smell them in the hall, long before they reached her room, and knew they were daisies.

Studying the daisies at her bedside, she laughed with delight at all the colors and patterns in the once white petals.

SECRET ORIGINS

People sometimes ask me why I don't write comic books. It's obvious I love comics, and have crammed far more superhero trivia into my brain than a normal skull should hold. I manage this by squeezing out less important information, like my siblings' birthdays or the names of coworkers I see every day.

Alas, I think the comic book industry has been damaged by the original sin of the earliest hit titles: The notion that all superheroes must exist as parts of series. Their stories can never end. Now, I think this is also true of some prose fiction.

I've committed trilogy and worse in my fantasy novels. Still, one reason I love writing superheroes in short fiction is that you can take one crisp, simple idea, explore it, then resolve it. When Stinger and Blue Bee die here, they get the dignity of not being resurrected and rebooted in a billion absurd variations. There's beauty in writing a story that actually ends.

EMPIRE OF DREAMS AND MIRACLES
ᔕᎧᏨᎧᏨᎧᏨᎧᏨᎧᏨᎧᏨᎧᏨᎧᏨᎧᏨᎧᏨᎧᏨᎧᏨᎧᏨᎧᏨᎧᏨᎧᏨ

I WOKE FROM a dream about technopaganneuro sex, unable to remember going to bed or what had happened to my clothes. I kicked aside the red silk sheets and sat up. On the silver table by my bed sat an antique toy, a black plastic ball with the number eight painted on its top. I couldn't remember where I had acquired it, but I vaguely recalled Rayn having described one to me once. Some sort of pre-technological oracle. Curious, I flipped it over. "HELL YEAH!" displayed in the milky window. The day was going to be a good one.

Energized, I jumped to the window and flung open the curtains. Warm sunlight and a salty breeze flooded the room. A young boy strolled by on the street below.

"You there!" I called out. "Young man! What day is this?"

"Put some clothes on," he yelled, and hurried along his way. He seemed very convincing, his stride, his expression. Perhaps he really was a boy. An original, I mean.

But original or copy, the oracle was already proving true. How Utopian to begin the day with a total stranger's kind advice.

Advice I promptly disregarded. I leapt from the balcony onto the brick pathway and ran toward the ocean. My body quickly warmed beneath the bright sun. I reached the beach and planted my toes in the hot white sand, stretching luxuriously as I cried to the smooth blue sky, "Good morning!"

And it was. I've never met a morning in Atlantis that wasn't simply brilliant.

I walked to my favorite ocean-side café and took a seat on the patio. The wait-thing brought me golden nectar and a black seaweed quiche. The wait-thing's transparent skin revealed internal clockwork, ceaselessly whirring.

A shadow fell across my breakfast. A deep, musical voice greeted me. "Good afternoon, Dobay."

It was Makan. You may know him. Big fellow, heavily muscled. Ebony skin, hair sculpted into a seahorse, florescent yellow lipstick and a single red feather through his Adam's apple. Not the sort of person who would stand out in a crowded room, but once you get past the mundane exterior you find a true creative genius. Makan's a deathpoet, one of the best.

"How's dying these days?" I asked.

"Same as ever." He shrugged, then took a seat. "You don't have any clothes on."

"Is that a problem?"

"Of course not. It's just you're normally so meticulous about your wardrobe."

"It's important to look good in public," I said.

"Well, you do."

"Thank you," I said. "I had a dream last night that will interest you. I was making love to a witchmachine, in a field of daisies..."

"Witchmachine?" he asked.

"A machine ," I said, perturbed by the interruption, "that's also a witch. Anyway, the thing slit my throat. It was a marvelous sensation. I grew lightheaded, my vision blurred. I could hear the rumble of blood as it left me, and felt every last bead of sweat that rolled across me."

"Yes," Makan said, toying with his throatfeather. "That matches my own experience with exsanguination. Borderline sexual, but difficult to climax."

"Rayn and Glantililly were talking about your drowning last week," I said. "I'm surprised you're back."

"Blame it on popularity," he said, shrugging. "When no one wanted to see me die, I had to stay gone years to build up buzz. Now, I get nine, ten requests a month. The price of fame."

"I think I killed someone last night," I said, then sipped my nectar. "Might have been messy."

"Oh?"

"Tough to know for certain. The absence of clothes is a good sign. Blood-soaked garments irritate me."

He nodded knowingly. "You seem calm about it."

"Can't get too worked up. It might throw me off."

"If you pulled off a murder, you're only one behind Faz Jaxxon."

"Drop it," I said. "Thinking about your score is a sure jinx."

"I'd best fly," said Makan. "I've got some prelim work to do with a shark. Most of them hate human blood."

"Then swap it," I said. "Seal blood, maybe."

"You know I'm a traditionalist," he said. He stood and leaned across the table. We kissed. His tongue was slimy and hard and tasted like ginger.

"Good luck with your killing," he said, as he floated skyward.

I wiped my mouth and looked at the glowing yellow smear on my hand. I'm glad he left. Talking about the game is bad luck. And I'm so primed to jabber.

BACK HOME, I sank into the womb and drifted awhile. There was never any doubt as to my destination, but I like to pretend I'm unconcerned. I slipped into a documentary about a place called America. Big place, chaotic, dangerous.

Hard to imagine the lack of control, the total absence of safety. You could die by eating the wrong thing, by walking on the wrong street, or, worst of all, by having your body just give out, betray you by becoming weaker and slower. When you died, that was it. No resurrection, just recycling. Worm food. Amazing we ever made it out alive.

Having spent enough time in the documentary, I slid over to the Game Show. Oh, yes. I did kill someone after all. I relived it, along with millions of others. There was a woman at my feet and I felt my shoulders burning, felt the smooth, wet knife in my hand, felt the rush of power that I get when I'm at the top of my game. But then I noticed her face, and all I could feel was shame. I knew this woman! The victim turned out to be Rayn, Glantililly's lover. What made me go for such an easy target? I knew she had registered as a victim; she'd talked about it for years. It's no sport to kill the ones who beg for it. Faz Jaxxon must have laughed himself wet.

I'd slipped in at the culmination, the most popular viewing time. My fellow citizens usually skip the hours of hunting and plunge right into the moment. I surfed backwards, past the break-in, past the stalking, until, ah... Glantililly. I could see her by my side as we strolled along the beach last evening near sunset. The fading light brought out the peacock iridescence of her hair, and the evening breeze played with the mist garment she wore, allowing enticing glimpses of the smooth violet curves of her body. We each carried a glass of Clear White Dreams (which explained my missing memory). We were talking about Rayn.

"It's her shield," said Glantililly. "By talking about her status, she knows hunters won't go for her. She registered for the thrill, but she's really afraid to die. She's a virgin."

"Incredible," I said. "I didn't know there were any left."

"It happens," Glantililly said. "She just never gave in to the curiosity when she was younger. Now she's all wrapped up in a tangle of fear and inhibition."

"Does she fear the pain?"

"It's more complex than that. I think she's afraid the reality of the moment will let her down, after all these years of imagining."

"Poor kid," I said. "Some people invest too much emotion in their first death."

"If only someone would help her get past this. Someone... experienced. Good at it."

I felt a glimmer of hope. Unable to wait any longer, I went straight to the scoreboard. My heart sank, then leapt. I scored only twelve points for the total kill, well below average, but half of it was in motivation, a six. It's difficult to get higher than a three in motivation anymore. There's so much competition, so much pressure to get another kill on the board to stay in the game, that there just isn't time to work up a real justification for murder. A six showed style.

Speaking of pressure, Faz Jaxxon had to be feeling it. I'd moved within three points. I was tempted to switch to his life to find out how far away he was from his next kill. Then I reminded myself I'm not in this for the score. I played the game because it sharpens my mind, strengthens my body, and enlarges my spirit. But, damn, three points!

I TOOK TO THE STREETS as shadows blanketed Atlantis. A magic breeze, salty and electric, danced through the streets to the beat of joyous music pouring from open doorways. Perhaps you know of such moments, such moods, when you realize you live in the Golden Age, that there is no better time or place to be alive than now, here, in the Empire of Dreams and Miracles.

I wore my finest white robes, scented with patchouli, my body freshly shaven and glowing with subdermal luminescence, a side effect of the hot pinks I'd popped before leaving my quarters. I carried my best knife in a sheath hidden in my left sleeve. It's a seven-inch blade, black ceramic, capable of cutting a hair lengthwise. I'm not superstitious. The knife isn't good luck. But fingering its bone hilt, I couldn't help but feel a sense of certainty. I would kill someone soon. A beautiful kill. Much better than a twelve.

Then I saw her. High above me, on the crystal bridge that crosses Garden Africa, she leaned against the rail, watching the sunset. She was dressed in black with long, flowing tresses. She had the air of one who might jump, should there be any point. World weary. Worn. Perfect. I hurried through the maze of stairs to reach her, hoping she would still be there by the time I reached the top.

She was. I placed myself beside her and looked out over the tan parklands. Zebras grazed by the lake, oblivious to the lions in the long shade of the boabab tree. She gave no reaction to my presence.

"Beautiful," I said.

"I know who you are," she said, her gaze still focused to the west.

"Oh?"

"Dobay the Gold. I've slipped into your life from time to time. Quite a show... for some."

"Thank you. I think. What's your name?"

"You try for something extra with your work."

"If a thing is worth doing..."

"Is anything worth doing?" she asked.

"Precisely anything," I said, intrigued by the turn in the conversation. I had been prepared for mindless banter about giraffes and such. "Anything at all, if you do it well."

"This is what eternity has reduced us to," she said.

For the first time, she turned her face toward me. Her eyes and lips were as black as her gown, in contrast with her pale porcelain skin. She smelled very alive, a musky odor that mixed well with the air from the park, very animal, very human.

"I didn't catch your name," I said.

"You get more points if I'm not a stranger," she said as she turned her gaze once more to the menagerie.

"I don't kill everyone I speak to," I said, feeling wounded. "It doesn't work like that."

"I know how it works," she said, with a dismissive roll of her eyes.

"Then you know you shouldn't assume things. People sometime prejudge me, imagine I size everyone up as a potential victim. But really, don't you think I just occasionally like to talk?"

"You could talk to, let's see, what's her name... Rayn?"

Suddenly, I understood. She was obviously a fan, disappointed that I had stooped to killing such an easy target.

"Rayn was an exception," I said, hoping to explain. "I don't kill inside my circle as a rule."

"Why not?"

I shrugged. "Things can be awkward afterward. Life's too long to have everyone be suspicious of you."

She turned back to me and smiled, an expression that didn't seem to fit her. Her lipstick changed color, becoming blood red.

"You're a philosopher," she said.

I am, but somehow it felt wrong to admit it.

"And a liar," she continued. "You did approach me with murder in mind."

"Believe what you want," I said.

"I've hurt your feelings," she said, with amusement. "Will you kill me for that?"

"Dream on." I snorted, and turned away. I had no time for her games. And you score no points at all if they ask for it.

THAT NIGHT I climbed the Bethlehem Spire and hung myself by the heels. Swaying for hours in the salt tanged breeze, Atlantis was my bright heaven, while beneath me spun the endless black night. I thought of Alandra.

The girl on the bridge had awakened her memory. It's true. Sometimes, after you kill someone, things change. Alandra was never the same. She drew away, closed herself in a womb, and was gone. So many years ago. I still ache for her. We were so young and serious. Everything had meaning.

But meaning was as fleeting as the shooting stars beneath my feet. I don't dwell upon the past. I realized long ago that even if a thousand stars fall each night for a thousand years, the sky will still twinkle with the promise of the infinite. In a world of infinite promise, how can I help but hold her again?

I MET MY FATHER for lunch. These days he's a she, just through puberty, blonde, pretty and completely unknowable. He calls himself Kandii.

"Have you spoken to your mother lately?" she asked.

"You know I haven't," I said. "You?"

She shook her head, then pushed her hair back from her eyes. Sometimes, I think I see him in her, in the faint ghost of one of his gestures. But he's fading. He's becoming his skin. I've seen him with boys, flirting, flaunting. It's hard to remember he's nine centuries old, old enough to have had a profession. He used to be a lawyer, but the world no longer needs laws. Maybe that's part of his identity crisis. Or maybe there's no crisis at all. Maybe it's just me who feels strange about this.

"I know you dislike confrontations," she said. "But I think we need to discuss your discomfort with what I've done."

"I'm not uncomfortable," I said. "It's your life."

"It is," she said gleefully. "And I've decided not to resist it any longer. I'm doing this to embrace every possibility. I'll be a man, a woman, old, young, a rainbow of colors. Any life we can imagine, we can have. A century from now, it will seem old fashioned to wake up in a body you've already worn."

She's probably right. In fact, I'm sure of it. It's the whole infinite promise thing. Why not keep it? If a thing can be done, do it. But I'm not ready. Not quite ready. Who can say? Maybe I'll never be ready to tell my father that I would gouge my eyes out for a chance to sleep with him. Oedipus had it so easy.

I SAW THE WOMAN from the bridge again that afternoon, on the Avenue of Yesterday. People seldom go there, but I went, knowing somehow I would find her. She wore white, and her hair was powdered to match. She looked like a living statue moving among the others. I followed her discreetly, certain she hadn't seen me. She seemed somnambulistic, oblivious even to the statues I thought she wished to emulate. What was wrong with this girl?

I felt a mix of pity and curiosity. How sad to be sad, I thought. Had someone she loved vanished? Was her longing like my own? Perhaps not. She seemed too cold, too distant to ever have loved, to ever have felt anything.

How would she respond to pain, to fear? Could I, with the strength in my hands and a single sharp blade, slice through the barriers that separated her from the desire to live? Could I awaken the flame inside her by smothering it?

Her "invitation" on the bridge was problematic. It was possible I might score no points for killing her. But, there was an ambiguity to the request. Certainly enough for an appeal if things went badly with the initial judges.

I stopped myself and shook my head, ashamed. What was I thinking? Killing a woman whose name I didn't even know for points? Where was my pride? I must make the kill not for my sake. Not even, in truth, for her sake, but for the kill's sake. It must be a single, perfect, enduring moment. That would be enough.

She left the Avenue of Yesterday, descending into the catacombs. This was where the uncounted billions of Atlantis spent most of their lives. There was far more to the city beneath the streets than above. We passed door after door, behind which our fellow citizens lay adrift in their wombs. Was she usually one of them? Was this only a temporary excursion into daylight? Was reality proving to be a disappointment?

She headed deeper, ever deeper, until the mechanical heart of the city itself could be heard, the vast engines that drove the clockwork of paradise. I had never explored this far down. We were nearing the forbidden area, and I wondered if she was heading toward it to destroy herself, for surely the city would only declare a place off limits if it contained dangers a human mind couldn't imagine. I was tempted to turn back, but pressed on.

The decorative tile work and murals of the upper sublevels were left behind. The passageways became shorter, the walls pale gray and smooth, with few places to hide. Devoting all my energies to remaining unseen, I realized I had grown quite lost. I had only her soft footsteps and scent of musk to guide me.

From ahead, a door clicked shut. I turned the corner and she was gone. The passageway ended with a door to my right, and another to my left. They looked ancient, made to resemble wood, with brass doorknobs green with age. I pressed my ear to the right entry. Nothing could be heard. I leaned against the left door.

Music. A violin, softly weeping.

I touched the knob. With a loud crack, a current of electricity shot through me. I fell, blacking out, amidst a shower of sparks.

I WOKE TO CANDLELIGHT. The room was tiny, the walls dark green and glistening, stretching up into gloom. I was naked, shivering from the chill of the concrete beneath me. I couldn't move my arms or legs. By straining my neck, I could see my limbs bound by strips of leather fastened to iron rings in the floor. The violin played more distinctly now, the solo from the *Plague Symphony* by Galacia. I never liked that song, with its terrible melancholy, though Makan had used it to great effect when burned at the stake.

"What's happening?" I asked, doubting I was alone.

"Something that matters," she answered, her voice drifting from somewhere high above.

"Is this a joke?" I asked.

A poorly greased wheel began to turn in the darkness. Her pale shape emerged slowly as she floated down, wraithlike, gaining corporeality as she grew closer, her skin bone-white, her lips and nails red as blood, her teeth gleaming. She was naked save for the elaborate leather harness that supported her. Her face tilted toward me and she kissed my forehead, a warm kiss, gentle. She looked into my eyes and told me, "This is the only serious moment you will ever live, Dobay the Gold."

"Oh, my," I said, with a grin. "I like the sound of it."

She came to rest upon me, her warm, moist crotch settling on mine, her long fingers stroking my hair. She slowly tickled her nails along my cheeks, down my neck, across my chest. Her hands vanished to my sides. I heard a scrape of metal against concrete. She raised her arms high overhead, brandishing an old fashioned hammer, the claw side toward me. And then, with a grunt, she swung.

I have no memory of the impact. I don't know if ten seconds or ten hours passed. My memory returns with my voice hoarse from shouting, my mouth filled with the taste of vomit, my sight half-gone. With each heartbeat, my pain grew more awful. I've broken almost every bone in my body over the years, but nothing compared with this. There were no pills to carry me forward, to mask or enhance my senses. I hurt, and she was stalking angrily about the room, cursing me.

"You are nothing but meat," she hissed.

I tried to speak, but my voice wouldn't come.

"What is it?" she demanded. "Answer me!"

I shook my head.

She kicked me in the groin, but the pain was like a cup poured into an ocean. And an icy ocean it was, draining from the pit of my stomach, sucking my pain and care into its undertow. I began to chuckle softly.

She knelt beside me and placed a finger on my lips.

"Shhh," she said. "Shhh."

"You'll get a lot of points for this," I whispered.

"Oh, darling," she said.

"We m-must share a drink — when I get back."

"Oh, my poor child," she said, her voice soft and tender. "You can't even imagine, can you? You aren't coming back."

It was difficult to focus on what she had said. But something rolled over inside my head. I felt myself swimming up through the cold tide.

"W-what's your name?" I asked.

"I am Death," she answered.

"Small world," I said. "I'm Dying."

"Not yet. You're a strong man."

She was right. The shock was wearing off, or perhaps just setting in. I realized how little pain I was truly feeling, how distant I was from my own body. This wasn't the best way to do it. Pain like this should be embraced, cherished, savored like fine wine. But I couldn't quite do it. I felt too focused on her. Jealous.

"I-I thought I knew all the other hunters," I said. "You m-must be new. What a d-debut."

"I've killed so, so many," she said. "I no longer count."

"I w-would have heard of you."

She shook her head. "I don't exist. Neither do you, anymore. My worms have eaten away all memory of you from the city's brain. There's no template left to rebuild you."

I didn't understand what she was getting at for several long seconds. When I did, I laughed.

"Oh, Death, you have such p-promise."

She sighed.

"But you've pushed it too far. Don't get me wrong. Most v-victims would get a nice jolt of fear from that."

"I don't want your fear," she said.

"Come on. It plays better that way. You score higher when the victim's really into it."

She answered me by slamming her heel down hard on my mouth, knocking teeth loose. She began to shout at me again.

"This is what everyone you kill has felt," she scolded. "Nothing but the physical. They aren't capable of real emotion. You disappoint me, Dobay. I thought there might be something more in you. Something human."

I spat out blood and teeth. I tried to revel in the pain, but couldn't. What was she trying to say? Why wouldn't she just shut up and let me suffer? I felt helpless in my confusion.

"What?" I cried. "What do you want from me?"

"After the struggle's done," she said, "all that's left is entertainment."

She crouched over me once more, her face close to mine. She lifted her hand to reveal my best knife. Laying the blade against my throat, she had that sad look again, the same look I had seen the first time I saw her. So weary, so worn. So alone.

She raised the blade.

There was a flash of light and a wet snick. Her head fell from her shoulders and bounced against my nose. Her body collapsed upon me, limp and wet. In the candlelight stood a man, red skinned, with a wild, black beard and a long, curved sword, blade dripping.

"Faz Jaxxon!" I laughed, with relief, with shock, and because his name just sounded stupid when spoken with my front teeth gone. "God damn you!"

He sliced my bonds with his sword, and helped me sit up against the wall. There was blood everywhere, but what was mine and what was hers I couldn't guess. One thing was clear through the haze, though.

"A rescue!" I couldn't believe it. "You'll max out on this one!"

"Whatever," he said. He knelt over Death, using his blade to slice off her ear. "Never think much about the points."

"No," I said. "Of course not. Me either."

"Oh?" he said, with a raised eyebrow. "You a hunter?"

"God, I must be a mess. I'm Dobay. Dobay the Gold."

"Huh," he said, placing the ear in a pouch on his belt. "Well, good luck, kid. Need some help getting to a womb? You don't look so hot."

"Fuck off," I said. "I don't need your help."

He smirked, then walked away.

"Good luck, kid!" I shouted as he turned the corner. "I'll have your ass!"

But instead of chasing after him, I chose that moment to faint.

NO ONE DISPOSED of her body. No one came to take me to a womb. I woke weak and feverish. The room was completely dark. The blood I lay in was thick and glue-like. With a gasp, I pulled my face free of the floor. I dragged myself away from that awful place. At last, I made it to the lighted hall.

"Help," I whispered. I lay on the cool floor, trying to make sense of what had happened. I had never felt so empty.

If I died, no doubt someone would come along soon enough and put me in a womb and I would be better. Even if someone only came this way once a year, even once a decade, what did it matter? I'd be good as new. I could escape this agony so easily. All I had to do was close my eyes and wait.

But I couldn't. Death had said she didn't want my fear, but she had it. In my weakened state, I was no longer sure. Maybe she could kill even my memory. If I closed my eyes — my eye — it might never open.

So I crawled, inch by inch, through the timeless shadows of the undercity. At last I reached a grotto with a small pool where I slaked my thirst and must have fallen asleep. I know that I woke hungry, but stronger. I was able to pull myself to my feet and limp along, with one hand upon the wall. I reached my home, but my door wouldn't open. I studied myself in its mirrored surface. Was this thing before me even human? One-eyed, scabbed, dirty, pale, gap-toothed...

But alive. Alive. And maybe that does count for something.

SUNRISES ARE MORE subtle than sunsets. I shivered on the beach, watching the black sky tint bloody. I wondered, if Makan were here, would he be jealous? Everyone likes to experience his deaths; he goes out of the way to insure the most torment, the most lucidity and pathos. But the way I felt that morning had a certain honesty to it, a sincerity Makan's choreographed agonies never attained. I grew proud of my pain. I couldn't wait to share it. And that, I think, was the key to my feeling that everything would work out.

The beauty of the world is that we go through nothing truly alone. Every moment of our lives, every deed and thought, can be shared by countless others, if we so choose. When I made it back into a womb and let myself free, everyone could feel as I felt, experiencing every ache and throb of my tortured flesh, sharing my emotions, my sense that the city had allowed this for a purpose, that this was all for the best. I felt a growing sense of importance as the sun arrived decisively, its eager rays dancing on my anguished skin. Something good was about to happen.

I looked around. I was alone on the beach, except for a distant figure, out for a morning stroll. She paused when she saw me, then continued. Soon I could see her skin was light green, and she wore a sky blue sarong. Her deep green hair danced like kelp in the steady wind. She carried a conch in her left hand.

It was her. She didn't look the same, true, but there was no doubt. I knew her walk, her lips, her eyes.

"Alandra," I said, as her shadow reached me.

"Do I know you?" she asked. Her voice was still the same.

"It is I. Dobay."

"Good morning, Dobay."

"You've changed your skin," I said. "It suits you."

"Thank you," she said, staring at my torn face. "But I'm not sure I understand your skin. Why have you done this? It must be painful."

I didn't know what to say. I wanted to tell her what had happened, to explain everything, but I couldn't. In all my countless dreams of reunion, I hadn't rehearsed those lines.

"This fashion eludes me," she said. "Why choose pain over comfort?"

Her words triggered my memory. "We've had this discussion before."

"Have we?"

"Long ago, after making love in the Plaza of Peace."

"I think you must be mistaken."

"No. I remember every word we ever spoke. I've relived them a hundred times."

"We've never met, Dobay."

"You're Alandra. Don't deny it."

"Yes."

"You must remember."

"This conversation holds no pleasure for me, Dobay. Enjoy your morning."

She looked away, further down the beach and began to walk.

"Wait!"

She placed the conch shell to her ear and didn't turn back.

I sat for the longest time, as my skin baked beneath the violent sun, my bones cold as ice.

WHEN I FELT stronger, I sought out Makan. It came as no surprise when he didn't know me. By that time, the truth of Death's words were becoming evident. How much of our self is us and how much is the city? If the city forgets you, you never existed. There is no food for you in the café. The lights don't brighten as you approach. The doors do not open.

But there was still fruit on the trees, and water, water everywhere. The city provided passively, if not actively. My fellow humans talked to me, however briefly. I think they thought I had gone too far. My ugliness, my malformed face... no one understood why I chose it. And the story I told, such a strange comedy, a theater of the absurd. Whenever they saw me again, it was for the first time. They didn't remember their promise to bring me clothing, or hot food, or blankets. They can't remember me. I must work to remember myself.

When I returned to Death, she still held my good knife. Beetles had stripped her to the bone. I hadn't known there were beetles outside the gardens. Perhaps the city doesn't know, either, or doesn't care. I took her skull. It was lighter than I would have imagined.

Now, I sit upon the western shore and contemplate the waves. Out there, they say, are continents, wild places, where men live as beasts. They were left behind when the city saved us. They rejected the promise of Atlantis, the promise of life without fear, without want, without end. Shunned by the city, they fell behind, devolving to hunters and gatherers, becoming prey to disease and dragons. There's no romance about it, despite the best efforts of our poets.

And we, the civilized... we're the city's pets. We're well fed, well groomed, healthy, loved. Out there, your hair is always tangled, your lungs wheeze, you dig in the dirt for your next meal, and insects dig into you for theirs. It's the promise of the finite. Out there, life kills you.

But not today, if I can help it.

My knife is tied around my neck with a leather cord. It's a good knife, the kind of knife a man might use to carve his name into a brand new world. I'm glad she kept it for me. I place my lips upon her teeth. If she could only see me now, scarred and lean and leathery, my hair wild about me. Would she recognize me? Would she understand? This is the end of my romance with Death. She brought me this far, but now I must leave her behind.

The sky is as red as the memory of her lips. The sun dances on the horizon, bringing morning to new lands. I dive into the waves, and chase the day.

SECRET ORIGINS

Before I wrote short stories, I wrote novels. First I wrote a "literary" novel about the meaning of life. It was wretched. Then I wrote a near future science fiction novel about genetically engineered dragons. It was called, creatively enough, *Dragons*. Then, I wrote a novel called *Bitterwood* that was set 1000 years after *Dragons*, when dragons ruled the earth and men skulked in the shadows as their prey. In *Bitterwood*, one of the dragons uses advanced nanotechnology, and I assumed he got it from humans who were still technologically advanced. But, the story wasn't about these humans, so I had only the vaguest notion about who they were or where they lived. The only mention of them in my original draft is when Vendevorex, the nanotech-using dragon, defeats a robot and says, "Hmm. I haven't seen one of these since I left Atlantis."

With that single line, I gave birth to my vision of a high tech paradise where civilized man had retreated to live in environmental isolation from the rest of the world. I tried writing a story about it where I showed it as a bleak dystopia where there was no privacy, where the lack of any real challenges in life had led to people coming up with creative ways to kill themselves. The story wasn't working, because it was basically 5000 words of people complaining about how terrible paradise was. It wasn't until I flipped my vision of the story, and decided to make my main character someone genuinely in love with Atlantis, that the real story came to me.

I waited a long time before I submitted this story to any markets. At the time, I felt like it was the best thing I'd ever written. I couldn't bear the thought of getting rejection letters for it. Luckily, I finally broke down and submitted it to the first Phobos awards contest. It was one of the twelve winners, and when those twelve stories were collected in an anthology, the book was called *Empire of Dreams and Miracles*. It was the first story where I was paid professional rates. Because of that, I often point to the publication of this story as the beginning of my career as an author.

RETURN TO SENDER
ഇ൫ൽ൫ഇൽൽൽ

I'M AT THE WINDOW, watching the dribble of traffic at two in the morning. In the dim reflection, Brother Anthony frowns as he studies the items spread out on the bed — various receipts, a few blurry pictures, handwritten notes. In his brown wool monk's habit, with the shaved tip of his scalp gleaming in the lamplight, he looks like a figure from the fifteenth century. He doesn't fit amid the modern furnishing in the penthouse of this high-rise hotel. He wears his otherness for everyone to see.

I place my hand on the window, my fingers meeting those of a matching phantom. My window-ghost stares as if she doesn't recognize me. I'm dressed in a Backgammon Pizza uniform — checkered shirt, navy pants, a cap with a bright red brim. My braid drapes over my shoulder and hangs down my chest like a black serpent. Like Sampson, I'm forbidden to cut my hair. But, even with locks down to my hips, I pass for an ordinary college girl with a side job delivering pizza. I look like I'm part of this world. It's only inside I'm so out of place.

Brother Anthony clears his throat. "This intelligence isn't very useful, Crystal." He picks up a white slip of paper. "What is this? ½ pep, sg, x chez?"

"That's the pizza order of the Golden Veil."

He furrows his brow, not fathoming the code. Pizza isn't on the menu at the monastery. I had my first taste only a month ago.

"Delivery driver may not have been the best cover," I say. "It's easy to get to Westcott's house, but I can't see much from the front door."

"Make conversation. Have them invite you inside." He offers this advice as if it's something I wouldn't have come up with on my own. I resist rolling my eyes.

"They would have been suspicious if I asked too many questions early on," I say. "Now they're used to me. It'll be easier to gain their trust."

I sound like I have some grand strategy. I'm clueless as to how to talk my way into the Golden Veil meeting house. The monks have trained me endless hours for combat, but never spent a single minute teaching me to make small talk. I know the true names of 3,333 angels, their realms and principalities, but don't know the name of a single professional sports team. Bill Westcott, the leader of the Golden Veil, gave me an opening on my second trip to his house. There was a football game on in the living room and he asked what team I rooted for. My brain locked up. All I know about football is that it's the sport where the ball isn't round.

"We're running out of time," says Brother Anthony. "It's two weekends until Halloween and we still don't know which of hell's minions the Golden Veil plans to summon."

"I'll go back next Saturday. They always order pizza. If they're up to something, I'll find out."

"You used the word, 'if,'" says Brother Anthony.

I anticipate a scolding.

"Crystal, our success depends on your unwavering faith. You cannot doubt for even a moment that your cause is just! These men will unleash a terrible evil into the world if you aren't vigilant."

"I know."

He doesn't look convinced.

My window-ghost isn't convinced either.

IT'S THREE IN THE MORNING when I get back to the dorm. I tiptoe into the room with the lights out so I won't wake my roommate. I stand for a minute in the darkness, listening to the silence. If Sherry's here, she isn't breathing. I flick on the lights and see her unmade bed.

Tension slides out of me. Sherry and I don't get along. What began as a lack of anything in common is festering into open hostility. She's a fashion conscious rich girl from Los Angeles. I'm the last Knight Templar, raised at a hidden monastery in Idaho.

Since Sherry's not here, I strip out of my Backgammon uniform and put on a robe, then kneel to begin my nightly prayers. I'm supposed to devote four hours a day to prayer, but I've been slipping without the monks' constant supervision. Prayer is good for anyone's soul, but in my case it has extra benefits.

According to the monks, my father is an angel named Baphomet. He's one of the good guys, a warrior spirit who stands ready to fight the final battle when Judgment Day arrives. Only, his vigilance has been known to waver, and he sometimes slips off to earth to relax in the company of humans — young, female humans in particular. For centuries, the Order of the Temple has tracked down Baphomet's bastard children and raised them as demi-angel soldiers, the Knights Templar. Through prayer I can tap into my angel blood and gain strength, toughness, and even a little magic. At least, that's the theory. Compared to the legends I hear about the feats of the knights of old, I don't feel all that strong or tough. The monks try to assure me that my magical gifts will kick in when they're truly needed; apparently a lot of other knights also got off to a slow start. I wish I had someone to talk to about this, but Baphomet has mostly behaved himself this century; there aren't any other half-angels around.

I've been praying for ten minutes when the door opens. It's Sherry; she's in a short black dress. A guy I don't know is standing next to her, his arm tight around her waist. She looks like she'd collapse without his support.

"Oh crap," she says, seeing me. "I thought you'd be asleep." Her speech is slurred.

"Are you drunk?" I ask. She's showing all the signs of inebriation the monk's have warned me about.

"What's it to you?" she asks. "Crystal, you gotta leave. Tim and I need to use the room."

"Jim," says the guy.

"Boys aren't allowed in the dorm at this hour. You could get expelled."

"No," she says, staggering toward me, "*you'll* get expelled." She giggles, apparently pleased with herself. "Hit the road. Tim and I have business."

"Jim," he says. "I don't mind if she stays."

I stand up. "Jim, you have to leave."

"You aren't my mom," says Sherry. "Get out of here!"

She grabs me by the arm and tries to pull me toward the door. It's a simple matter to use the momentum of her tug and separate her from Jim. I spin her around and launch her toward the lower bunk with a gentle shove. She lands face down on her pillow.

I put my hands on my hips and give Jim a stern stare. "You're going to leave now."

"She invited me."

"I'm uninviting you." Then, though he's taller than me by a foot, I grab him by the throat with both hands, lift him from his feet, and carry him back into the hall. I drop him on his butt and say, "Have a good night," as I close the door.

I don't know if that was angel strength or adrenaline, but it felt pretty good.

Sherry is still in the bed, face down, giggling.

"Alcohol lowers your inhibitions," I say, wondering how she can be unaware of this. "It's extremely dangerous, not to mention illegal at our age."

She sighs, still face down. She looks completely limp, too worn out to move. She mumbles something.

"What was that?" I ask.

She turns her head slightly. "You're such a buzzkill."

I've not heard the word before, but it's easy enough to decipher from the context. I'm ready to lecture her, to point out how many different dangers she's inviting to both body and soul, when I realize that she's passed out.

Out in the hall, footsteps stumble away. Jim dissuades easily.

Too bad. It might have been fun to really pound him.

WHILE I'VE HAD a lot of training, this is my first mission in the "real" world. The monks keep track of various supernatural threats, and the latest thing on their radar is a cult called the Golden Veil. The group was founded in Victorian England; it's waxed and waned over the years, vanishing completely for a few decades before a history professor named Bill Westcott started it back up.

My role as a student is the monk's way of hiding me in plain sight so I can keep tabs on Westcott. My job at Backgammon Pizza takes me straight to his living room every Saturday night. A side benefit of delivering pizza is that I get to pretend to be normal for whole hours at a time. My visits to the Golden Veil take only a few minutes. The rest of the night I'm bringing pizzas to rowdy college dorms and quiet, middle-class neighborhoods. Despite my inability to make small talk, I earn good tips. Mostly, I've been spending my money on music.

The background music at Backgammon is something called "oldies," though it's all new to me. I'm fond of this one singer called Elvis. I can't get enough of "Heartbreak Hotel." Of course to be heartbroken, I'd have to fall in love, and that's not going to happen. Romance, the monks tell me, would be the end of me. Like Sampson, I've got a list of no-nos as long as my arm. Sampson was done in by carnal desires. Fortunately, having grown up surrounded by pasty-faced monks, the needle on my carnal desire meter rests safely on "E."

IT'S THE LAST Saturday before Halloween. The Golden Veil meets at 9:00 p.m.; the pizza order comes in at 9:05. It's always one large pie, half pepperoni, half sausage, extra cheese. The fact that it's one pizza is useful intelligence. Westcott doesn't have many followers.

I'm humming "Blue Suede Shoes," as I get out of my car. Westcott lives in a Victorian house, surrounded by high hedges. No grass grows in the yard; there's too much shade from the giant oaks that hide the front of the house. The place has seen better days. It's ringed by a wide porch that wraps all the way around, gray paint peeling, the boards split, rusty nail heads jutting up along the edges. I rap on the door. It's mostly glass, but I can't see inside due to a lace curtain, yellowed with age. As I wait, I softly sing, *"uh-uh honey lay off of my — "*

"Is that Elvis?" a voice behind me asks.

I spin around. Westcott is standing at the foot of the stairs. He has a small black Chihuahua on a leash. The dog growls and bares its teeth, his eyes narrow little slits.

"Didn't mean to startle you," says Westcott. "Hercules and I were at the hedge when you walked past. You were singing Elvis?"

"Yes sir."

Westcott smiles. He's sixty years old, tall but with hunched shoulders. He has a gentle smile and soft blue eyes. His hair is perfectly combed, and his cheeks have no trace of razor stubble. The most sinister thing about him is his complete lack of menace. He doesn't look like the leader of a cult planning on summoning a resident of hell.

He says, "I made a joke about Elvis in class and no one got it. Made me feel ancient."

"What was the joke?"

"I was lecturing on the roman emperor Elagabalus, about how he died in a latrine. Said I could write a book on famous people who died in their bathroom; Elvis would be chapter twenty."

He smiles.

Was that the whole joke? I force myself to grin.

Westcott sighs. "Not that funny?"

"I just… I don't know much about Elvis. He's dead?"

Westcott laughs as he walks onto the porch. "Oh lord. Now I really feel old."

"Don't go by what I know. I had a sheltered childhood."

He nods. "I noticed the hair, and you're not wearing makeup. I had the impression you were a hippy, but now I'm guessing you're a fundamentalist?"

"Sort of," I say, annoyed that he feels so free to label me.

He winks at me. His eyes fall to my chest. This makes me uncomfortable until I realize he's reading my nametag. "We'll keep your Elvis fetish our little secret, Crystal. Come in while I get my wallet."

I step into the foyer. Three older men are sitting in the living room, just ten feet away. As Westcott goes into the room, I follow, and ask, "Is this your bridge night?"

"Poker, actually."

The living room is huge. There's a big fireplace and tall windows covered in curtains that have seen better days. Two beat-up leather couches face across a low, wide coffee table covered with dusty mail. Westcott was divorced ten years ago; it looks like it's been that long since anyone's vacuumed.

"Next weekend's Halloween," I say, searching for an opening. "What a great house for a party."

Westcott shrugs as he walks toward me, counting money. "I'm afraid my party days are behind me."

"He'd have to clean up if he had a party," jokes a short, dumpy man on one of the couches. I know him from my briefings as Scott Patterson, owner of Patterson's Pages, a used book store.

An idea pops into my head. "You know, pizza delivery is only one of my jobs. I also do maid work. My fees are really reasonable."

In a perfect world, Westcott would smile and ask what I charged. I could ask to see more of the house to form an estimate. Instead, he frowns. "I didn't invite you in to criticize my housekeeping."

The Chihuahua next to him is still growling, his pointy body aimed like an arrow as he eyes my ankles.

"I didn't mean any offense."

"None taken." Westcott hands me money. "Keep the change."

He takes the pizza from me and heads for the door. I see no choice but to follow.

"Good night," he says as he shuts the door behind me.

I look at the money. He's tipped me sixty cents.

DRIVING BACK to Backgammon, I weigh my options. Westcott's schedule is public knowledge; I'll have to break into his home when he's in class. Brother Anthony wanted me to take this approach a month ago. But, this is my first time living on my own, away from the monks. If I'd wrapped up this mission a month ago, I'd be back in the monastery now. I'm kind of enjoying playing college girl. I may not like my roommate, but at least my vocabulary is getting richer because of her.

At the end of my shift I clock out without talking to anyone. As a driver, I spend more time out of the restaurant than in it. I barely know the names of my coworkers. They frequently hang out around the back but I've never joined them. I don't have any friends my age. I don't have any friends at all, just trainers and handlers. Still, friendship isn't on my list of forbidden temptations. I'd love to find someone I could talk to about… well, about anything. I could tell them about angels and they could tell me about Elvis. But my coworkers behind the restaurant are poor candidates for companionship. They're always smoking. Tobacco is on my list of "thou-shalt-nots."

I walk past the schedule posted next to the time clock without paying it much attention. Then I step back and look closer. I'm not scheduled for next Saturday. I've been swapped with Jason to work Friday night.

I find Skater, the assistant manager, out back. He's only a year older than I am, but isn't a student. He's been working here full-time since he was seventeen. He's a few inches taller than me, athletic in a skinny way, with spiky black hair and a constellation of silver studs in both ears. His left arm is covered in tattoos, heavy black stripes in a tiger pattern. I've never seen him outside the restaurant without a cigarette in his mouth.

Skater is talking to Brandy, another driver, but their conversation is wrapping up.

"See you Monday," Brandy says as she walks toward a beat up Honda Civic. Skater flicks the remnants of his cigarette to the pavement, then turns to go back inside, nearly running into me.

"Woah," he says. "Didn't see you, Crystal."

His breath smells sweet, like cloves, instead of ordinary cigarettes.

"Why am I switched with Jason?" I ask. "I always work Saturdays."

He shrugs. "Jason's band has a gig Friday at the Cool Brew. Wanna go?"

"I'm working Friday! That's the point of this conversation."

"Oh, right. No problem. They won't get on stage 'til after midnight."

"Then why switch us?"

"He said please."

I cross my arms. "I can only work Saturdays."

"Then I'll get someone else to cover Friday, and you can have Saturday off. Brandy's having a Halloween party. You wanna go to it with me?"

"She hasn't invited me."

"I'm inviting you."

My thoughts skid to a sudden halt. Is he asking me out? "I... uh—"

Skater jumps in, saving me from one awkward moment by plunging me into another. "I mean, hey, it doesn't have to be, like, a date. I understand if you aren't into men."

My cheeks flush red. "I... what are you implying?"

He looks at his feet, embarrassed. "Wow, I'm really blowing this. Sorry. You're tough to read, Crystal. You're so quiet."

"I'm just shy," I say, pushing a stray strand of hair back from my face.

"So... you wanna go to the party with me, shy girl?"

"Why would you ask me out? You don't know anything about me."

He shrugs. "You're mysterious. I like mysteries."

"I'm not mysterious. I'm boring."

"I'm not picking up that vibe," he says, looking directly at my face. "Here's a wild guess: I bet you were home-schooled."

"You might say that."

"I was too! My mom and dad are religious freaks. They went to this crazy church. It's why I moved out of the house when I was seventeen."

I frown. "What church?"

"The Pentecostal Assembly of Signs. It has, like, twenty members, all snake handlers."

"Snake handlers?"

"They shall take up serpents; and if they drink any deadly thing, it shall not hurt them. They play with venomous snakes

during worship. I was barely out of diapers before I started picking up snakes myself. But, when I was fourteen, one day I looked down at the copperhead in my lap and thought, 'Holy shit! This is insane!' My faith never recovered from that moment of clarity. Eventually, I was kicked out of the church, then kicked out of my family."

"I'm sorry."

"I'm not. I've got my own job, my own place, my own life. I'm broke half the time, but I get by. My folks used to warn of the evils of the world; most of those evils are a lot of damn fun. How about you, Crystal? What are your parents?"

"Um... catholic," I say. Which is a lie; the church considers the Order of the Temple heretical. But telling him my father is an angel and my mother was a stripper in Vegas doesn't seem prudent.

"You still religious?" he asks.

"I guess."

"That doesn't sound like a ringing endorsement."

I shrug.

"Religious or not, you can still party, right?"

"I'm not sure I can. I definitely don't drink."

"Hey, neither do I," he says. "Can't stand the smell of beer. Clove cigarettes are my only real vice."

"Cigarettes of any kind are dangerous."

"What are you, the Surgeon General?" He rolls his eyes. "All fun things are dangerous. If you tried to avoid everything bad, you'd have to seal yourself off in a monastery. Who the hell wants that?"

I want to answer, "Not me," but hold my tongue. It's disturbing how quickly these words spring into my head.

I TOLD SKATER I'd think about going to the party, not really intending to. But, two days later, the entire conversation keeps playing in my mind as I walk across Westcott's backyard in broad daylight. I envy Skater; in a way, he's lucky to have been raised by people with such outlandish beliefs. It must have made it easy to break free from their control. I don't have that luxury. I suppose I should be grateful to have been stolen from my cradle by monks who taught me the truth of my angelic heritage instead of being raised by members of some weird cult.

Westcott teaches at 1:30. I have at least an hour. The high hedges block me from sight as I reach his back door. It takes about thirty seconds to pick the lock to his kitchen.

Alas, I'd forgotten about the Chihuahua; the little ankle-biter charges into the kitchen and immediately starts biting my ankles. I snatch him by the scruff of his neck before he can draw blood. He sprays my arm with dog spittle as he snarls. I pull open the oven door, toss him inside, then slam it shut.

With the dog out of the way, I'm free to search the house. I start with the piles of documents on the living room coffee table. Everything proves mundane — papers from the college about changes to an insurance plan, an invitation to a classical history conference, a letter from NPR thanking Westcott for his recent donation, and mounds of junk mail.

I leave the table, realizing that I'll never be able to read everything in time. Really, what am I looking for? A confession scrawled in blood? The receipt the devil gave Westcott for his soul?

Upstairs, the master bedroom is a mess. The man doesn't bother to pick up his socks or underwear. Half of the king-sized bed is piled with books and magazines. Coffee cups are stacked on the windowsill. The room smells strongly of dog.

On the wall, there's a photograph; a much younger Westcott stands next to a woman. Disturbingly, her face has been scratched off. At some point, the photo has been removed from the frame and arrows and knives riddling the woman's torso have been drawn in with a ballpoint pen. From what I've read, Westcott's ex-wife pretty much got everything but the house in the divorce. I suppose mangling her photograph isn't that strange, though reframing it and hanging it above the bed does seem a little unhealthy. Still, it's hardly evidence of black magic.

I open the bedroom closet, and my heart skips a beat. A black robe hangs in a clear dry-cleaning bag. I pull it out, barely believing my eyes. The classic image of an evil cultist is a man in a hooded black robe. Westcott is living up to the cliché! Only, the robe doesn't have a hood. Instead, there's a square hat with a tassel in the same bag. Suddenly, it hits me: This *is* a ceremonial robe — graduation ceremony.

The rest of the hour is equally fruitless. A set of old, leather-bound books proves to be by Charles Dickens rather than Aleister Crowley. The cellar holds picks and shovels... and rakes and hoes and other gardening tools. There's a freezer big enough to hold a body. Mainly it holds steaks and corn-on-the-cob.

With time to spare, I yank the dog from the oven and fling him toward the couch in the next room as I bolt for the backyard. Two seconds after I close the door there's a thump as the dog hits it, barking wildly.

I shake my head as I stroll away. The devil-dog is the only real evidence that Westcott is in league with evil. What if the monks are wrong about him? What if they're wrong about a lot of things?

BROTHER ANTHONY SCRATCHES his scaly scalp as he reads my report.

"Perhaps the dog is a familiar?" he says.

"Perhaps the dog is a dog."

"That doesn't change the basic case against Westcott. He's a direct blood descendent of Wynn Westcott, the original founder. He's inherited all the scrolls and magical relics of the order. Then there's Patterson, the book dealer, who purchased the only surviving copy of the *Gibbering Codex*. And, most damning, we have the intercepted emails, pointing to a summoning this Saturday."

"About those emails. Why haven't I seen them?"

"They would only distract you. It's not as if they openly discuss their plans. Brother Bacon is still working to unlock the code phrases of the sect. Until then, we —"

"What if there are no codes?"

Brother Anthony furrows his brow.

"What if you've intercepted innocent emails and are so determined there's a code that you read things into them?"

"This is no time for doubt. We know what Westcott intends. The *Gibbering Codex* contains instructions to open a gate directly to hell and pull forth its most dreaded spirits. We know this requires the prayers of thirteen unholy men, the sacrifice of a virgin, barren soil, and the psychic energies unleashed by millions of revelers on Halloween. You have yet to make progress on any of these leads."

I throw my hands into the air. "Maybe there's no progress to be made! First, there aren't thirteen guys. It's just four old men who say they play poker. As for sacrificing a virgin, I've been reading the papers. Unless they have a volunteer, they'd need to kidnap someone, and no one around here has gone missing. Barren soil? Westcott's yard fits the bill, I guess. But I'm not willing to chop a man's head off because he's got a bad lawn."

"The threat —"

"If Westcott is so dangerous, why don't we call the police?"

Brother Anthony frowns. "Ordinary legal authorities won't understand the evidence. They would —"

I hold up my hand, not letting him finish: "If we went to them, we'd sound crazy. Because it is crazy. Everything you've ever told me is crazy."

Brother Anthony looks shocked. I'm surprised that I've said it as well. But, now that it's out in the open, I have no regrets. I feel — how did Skater put it? — my moment of clarity.

I've been raised by men who admit they kidnapped me. I've been told my father is an angel. And, yeah, I've seen some things that are hard to explain. Things I thought for certain were supernatural. But magicians pull rabbits out of hats and saw women in half. Little kids believe it's magic.

I'm not a little kid anymore.

Brother Anthony composes himself and says, "You're behaving like a child, Crystal. If you're done with your tantrum, we need to discuss the plan for Halloween."

I head toward the door and don't look back. "I already have plans."

ON FRIDAY, I go to the concert with Skater. It's a musical style called "thrash." Elvis didn't prepare me for this. The noise pumping from the speakers is pure chaos. I can't discern a melody. The only thing musical about it is the muddled pulse of bass beats.

I kind of like it.

"It reminds me of the music in my church," Skater yells.

"You had a bass guitar in your church?" I shout back.

"Sure! Drums, keyboard, the works. Men would run around the sanctuary on the backs of pews, possessed by the Holy Spirit. Turns out, they were just possessed by rock and roll."

We wander around the club. Skater knows everyone. People smile and speak to me; mostly I just nod, since the noise makes conversation tricky. A girl in torn blue jeans offers me a plastic cup full of beer. I think it over for thirty seconds, then take a sip. Skater's right; it tastes awful. Even though I swallow instead of spit, I don't feel any different. This is what the monks were so afraid of?

Later, we pass an all-night diner as Skater walks me back to the dorm. It's four in the morning and I'm wide awake. We go in and sit at a booth and I have my first cup of coffee. It's horrible! It's my second forbidden-fruit of the night, and the second let-down. I watch as Skater augments his cup with heaping spoons of sugar and three packets of cream. I try the same approach. The coffee turns sweet and milky, the residual bitterness a tickle on my tongue instead of a violent assault. This is good enough it must be sinful.

It's dawn when we reach my dorm. At some point my hand has slipped into his. He pulls me close and leans his face toward mine, his eyes closed. My first kiss doesn't go smoothly. I keep my eyes open, worried our mouths will miss. Skater's stubbly mustache is like sandpaper, but his lips are soft and sugary. His clove cigarettes make them taste like I imagine candy must taste.

I've never had candy.

What better day to get my hands on some than Halloween?

SATURDAY AFTERNOON, after a day of fitful sleep, I visit Wal-Mart. I stare at the costumes, bewildered. I recognize the witches and vampires, but have no clue what a Darth Vader is. It's lucky Westcott didn't have one of these in his closet.

I buy a nurse costume. Pretending to be someone doing good in the world makes more sense than pretending to be a witch. The costume has an impractically short skirt. I pick up a pair of tights to go with the outfit.

Then I put the tights back.

I go to the toiletries section and find a package of pink razors. I'm forbidden to cut my hair, no matter where it might grow.

As night falls, I spend an hour in the shower, shaving my legs. It's a painful experience, but once I'm halfway done with the left calf, there's no turning back. The right leg goes better. A few nicks, but it doesn't look like I've been crawling across barbed wire. The smoothness beneath my fingertips is strange and thrilling. I smile as I think about Skater's reaction.

After I get dressed, I stare at myself in the mirror, bouncing between excitement and mortification. I've tried applying make-up. The lip-stick looks good, but I'm not certain the eye-liner works. That's the least of my worries; the nurse's outfit is the most revealing thing I've ever worn. With my exposed cleavage and bare legs, I feel naked. On the other hand, I've been strenuously exercising since I could walk. My body is taut and toned, a living sculpture I've sweated untold hours to polish. Why shouldn't I show it off a little?

Despite my internal pep talk, I cringe as the door opens and reach for my trench coat. It's Sherry. She's alone and, to my relief, looks sober. I barely see her any more; she's been avoiding me since I kicked out Tim. Jim. Whoever.

Her eyes widen as she catches sight of me in the revealing outfit. Before I can cover up she says, "This is a new look for you, church girl."

I put on the coat. "I'd stick around to let you tease me, but I'm running late."

She smiles faintly as she looks me over. "I had no idea you were so ripped. I thought Jim was crazy when he said you picked him up. But, you look good. You should show your legs more often."

"Oh. Thanks." I glance at the clock, feeling nervous. Is she complimenting me to set me up for an insult? "I really am running late."

She's standing in the doorway. I need her to move so I can leave. But she just lingers there, looking like she has something else to say. She presses her lips tightly together and breathes deeply through her nose. Then, she relaxes, and says, "Look, about Jim... I... I'm sorry."

I tilt my head, not certain I've heard her correctly.

"I never drank that much before," she says, shaking her head slowly. "I kind of don't remember the details. But, to hear Jim tell it, you were ready to kick his ass."

"I'd had a long day," I say. "I hope I didn't hurt him."

"You don't have anything to feel sorry about. I was out of control that night. I'd only just met Jim. Now, I've had a chance to talk to him, and, honestly, he's kind of a creep. I'm embarrassed that you cared more about me that night than I did. This isn't easy for me to say, but, thank you."

"You're welcome," I say, still wondering if this is a joke. "Does this mean we aren't enemies anymore?"

"Definitely." Then, in a hesitant tone, "Maybe we'll even be, you know, friends."

"I'd like that."

"Good," she says. Then, she looks at my face with a critical eye. "It's a duty of friends to be honest, and honestly Crystal, your make-up looks awful. Take your coat off. Your date can wait ten more minutes. I'll have you all dolled up in no time."

SKATER DOESN'T DRIVE, so I'm supposed to pick him up. It's almost nine when I leave the dorm, pitch dark and chilly. The wind on my bare legs makes me wish I'd bought the tights. I can't wait to turn on the heat in my car. I look into my purse, finding my keys. When I look up, there's a red and white dishrag rushing toward my face. I release a stifled scream as a large, strong hand smashes the damp cloth against my mouth. An arm wraps around my waist from behind and jerks me from my feet. I suppose I should fear for my life, but all I can think of is that this idiot's going to smudge my make-up.

Whoever my attacker is, he's in for a surprise. I bring my elbows back in swift, hard jabs, connecting with ribs. My attacker grunts, but doesn't lose his grip. Since he's holding me in the air, I raise both legs high, then snap them back, my heels connecting with my assailant's knee caps. Something pops and we topple. He screams as his grip goes loose. I take a deep gasp.

Immediately, I go dizzy. The rag is still near my face, drenched with ether. I cough violently as footsteps charge toward me from a half dozen directions. People rushing to help?

Yes, but not to help me. A hand grabs the dishrag and pushes it back to my lips as strong fingers close around my wrists and ankles. I struggle, freeing a hand, but succeed only in smashing my knuckles into pavement.

Against my will, I inhale. The world spins as the sickly chemical air washes into my lungs. I breathe again, and fade. Distant voices. A dozen rough hands upon me. Spots dance before my eyes. My last ember of awareness smolders, then goes dark.

I FLICKER BACK toward consciousness. I open my eyes, but can't see anything. My arms are tied behind my back. I'm lulled by the soft rumble of wheels on pavement. Am I in a trunk? The air is still thick with ether. Slowly, I drift... back... out.

FRESH AIR WASHES over me. Hands grab my ankles, another pair slips into my armpits. I crack open my eyes and see a man pouring liquid from a brown bottle onto the dishrag. I try to speak, but the man turns, in slow, dreamlike motion, and drapes the rag over my face like a shroud.

I cannot fight the embrace of nothingness.

FLASHES OF AWARENESS: Cold scissors against my ribs as my clothes are cut away, followed by a cold, silent, void. A glimpse of three men in black robes, whispering gibberish, trailing off to nothing. I rouse to the sound of a small dog snarling, then hear a murmured conversation.

"You've confirmed she's a virgin?"

"The doctor's sure of it."

"Sheeeeeeessss perrrrfect...."

The voices retreat as I slide down an oily black vortex, never to return...

... AND THEN I come back, my spirit clawing into my body inch by precious inch. I'm not lying down any more. My arms are numb; I'm hanging from my wrists. I'm freezing, stark naked. My jaw aches from the cloth stuffed in my mouth. It takes all my strength to open my eyelids. I'm in what looks like an airplane hanger, the concrete floor covered with oil stains. There's a chalk pentacle drawn on the floor, at least ten yards across. Candles gutter at the points, the only light.

I crane my neck. My back is pressed against a steel girder. My wrists are bound by a thick rope which vanishes into the darkness above me. My legs are also tied. I probe the obstruction in my mouth with my tongue; it has to be the dishrag. The ether has mostly evaporated, but I'm still fuzzy enough not to feel panic. My whereabouts seep into my brain in a cool, matter-of-fact way.

I take a deep breath through my nose. The cold air slices my sinuses. The pain helps me focus. I've been trained to escape from ropes. I just need a few minutes to get my strength back.

I don't get them. A large door rumbles open; an icy wind hits me a few seconds later. Pinpoints of light appear in the darkness. Thirteen shadows advance toward me, carrying candles. They're chanting, a babbled mix of Latin, Hebrew, and Greek. The men are all anonymous beneath their hoods, but as they reach the pentacle my eyes spot a familiar figure. The thirteenth man doesn't carry a candle. He's carrying Westcott's dog. Little Hercules is silenced with a muzzle of twine. His legs are also bound. The dog shivers, helpless, as the thirteenth man places him in the center of the star.

Ten of the men take positions around the star, five standing at the outer tips, five standing at the junctions where the lines cross. They kneel prayerfully, their foreheads to the ground, arms outstretched toward the Chihuahua.

The dog carrier, the procession leader, and the man behind him all approach me. I can see their mouths and chins beneath the shadows of the hoods, and recognize two of the cultists. It's no great surprise that the leader is Westcott. He draws a long, gleaming knife from his belt. Patterson stands next to him. He's carrying a heavy, leather-bound book with iron hinges. The third man pulls a silver bowl from the folds of his robe. My heart seizes as he looks up at me.

Skater.

Patterson opens the book and begins to read. The words of the *Gibbering Codex* are a long string of nonsense, random syllables, grunts, and clicks. This is going to be a very stupid way to die. Yet, fear of impending death isn't the worst thing going on in my head. The worst thing is feeling like a complete idiot. I thought Skater liked me. He's been playing me all along and I fell for it.

I can't believe I shaved my legs for him.

Then Westcott stabs me.

The blade slides in just beneath my belly button, digging deep as he draws a long, curved line toward my ribs. Pain jangles along my spine; sweat erupts from every pore. I arch my back, banging my head against the girder. Despite the gag in my mouth, I scream. It comes out as a low, long groan.

Unable to inhale, I go limp, my head dropping forward. My blood spills into the silver bowl. It fills with disturbing speed.

When the bowl overflows, the three men turn and walk toward the dog. I can barely lift my head. White stars spark at the edge of my vision. The roar in my ears drowns out the chanting.

Skater kneels before the Chihuahua. Westcott bows down, untying the dog's twine muzzle. Hercules is too terrified to make a sound as Westcott shoves the dog's mouth into the bowl.

All color drains from the world. I'm staring down a gray tunnel at Hercules, who kicks and wiggles as he drowns in my blood.

The dog swallows.

Then grows. And grows. The three men step back as the twine bindings snap. Hercules is on his back, twitching, as he swells to the size of a Saint Bernard. I raise my head higher, forcing myself to watch. Now he's the size of a horse, rolling over onto his feet. He whines and whimpers. The dog's shoulders bulge as tumors like twin watermelons grow beneath his skin. Eyes open near the back of the tumors, followed by sprouting ears. There's a sickening rip as the bulges split open, revealing mouths. Hercules is now the size of a Brahma bull, with three heads and six eyes that glow red like brimstone.

It's Cerberus.

They've summoned Cerberus.

They've made a terrible, terrible mistake.

Since leaving the monastery, my faith in the monk's teachings has slipped away, nibbled and gnawed by the modern world until it was easy to believe that my own absurd, impossible history was all a lie.

If I were completely human, I'd be dead by now.

I turn my eyes toward heaven. *Father*, I pray, silently. *I need your strength.*

It's not God I'm praying to.

I feel a jolt rush through me and I'm no longer cold. I'm full of hot lighting, my heart thundering in my ears. The hemp rope tying me to the ceiling snaps like kite string. I fall forward, my feet still tied to the girder. I kick, breaking free, then bite through my gag and spit it out.

Grasping my belly, I rise to my feet. Loops of intestine slip out, suspended in my fingers. I clench my teeth as I push my guts back inside.

Cerberus is the size of an elephant. No one is looking at me. Westcott raises his hands and informs hell's guard dog that he's been summoned to serve and obey. He holds up a photo of his ex-wife.

"Your first mission is to find this woman and kill her."

Cerberus responds by nosing forward, opening the jaws of his left head, and crushing Westcott's skull like an egg. For a half second, the other twelve men fall silent, staring as Westcott's body wobbles, then topples backward.

Everyone runs. Most make it to the door, but not Patterson, and not Skater. I feel what must be heartache as the big dog gulps down the only boy who ever kissed me. I'd hoped to feel the stubble of his face again, when I pummeled him to within an inch of life.

Cerberus jumps out of his summoning circle. I've got to send him back. The three-headed hound dog isn't stationed at the gates of hell to keep people out. He's there to keep the damned in. Once they realize he's gone, the world will be overrun with vengeful, insane spirits. *Happy Halloween*.

I spin around and place my hand on the girder. I whisper a prayer that has appeared in my head as if by divine inspiration and the girder melts like a candle. Cold liquid iron flows down my arm and across my torso. I pull my hand away as the metal covers my belly and stiffens. At least I won't be tripping over my own entrails.

As the iron flows over my legs, I flex my right hand, summoning steel into it, forging a sword by sheer willpower. I bring the fresh iron to my lips and kiss the blade. The fever heat in my blood jumps into the metal; with a *WHOOSH* it bursts into white flame.

I jerk my head forward and the faceplate of my just-formed helmet drops into place with a satisfying clang. With a rapid prayer of thanks to my angel dad, I run forward, brandishing my sword, unleashing a battle cry as Cerberus hunches down to slip out the open doorway.

He spins around, bloody spittle foaming in his jaws, snarling as he sees me. He lunges, faster than my eyes can track. One second, he's ten yard away, the next, he's got a set of jaws clamped around my left thigh and his middle mouth chewing on my ribs. His third jaw goes for my wrist, to make me drop the angel blade, but now it's time to surprise him with my own speed. His jaws snap down on the foundry-hot steel of my sword and all three mouths turn loose as he jerks away, yelping.

"Bad dog!" I shout, jamming the gauntleted fingers of my left hand into the nostrils of his middle head as deep as they will go. I hook my fingers up and he howls, shaking his heads violently. I stand firm as Gibraltar, clamped down on his nose, immune to his fury.

With angel blood powering my muscles, I drag him back toward the pentacle. I'm not sure what I'll do when I get him there. If I kill him, it might leave hell wide open. The left head keeps snapping at me, but the right head hangs back, its mouth still smoking from its flaming-sword snack. My armor resists the worst of the left head's assault, but his hell-dog slobber feels like battery acid as it seeps through the joints.

I hum "Hound Dog," as I drag him over the smooth concrete floor, his claws leaving long scratch marks.

I get Cerberus back in the middle of the pentagram at the part of the song where the dog is scolded for his failures as a rabbit-catcher. I slap the right head across the nose with the flat of my blade, then twist my fingers deep in the middle head's nostrils. The left head yowls.

"Listen up," I say, going for the direct approach. "I could try all night to guess the magic words that send you back. Or, I can just keep hurting you until you've decided you've had enough. In hell, you get to hurt people. Here, I get to hurt you. This should be an easy choice."

The dog stops struggling, his six eyes glowering as he studies me. He sighs. A shudder ripples along his body.

I blink.

When my eyes open I'm sure that he's a little smaller. Five seconds later, there's no question that he's smaller still.

Before I know it he's no bigger than a German Shepherd. Waves of dark energy swirl around me, toilet bowl fashion, as the hell-spirit departs the dog flesh and heads back home.

I'm left with a dazed, bloody-nosed Chihuahua hanging from my fingertips. He whines pitifully, his whole body limp, as I pull him off.

My armor is suddenly very heavy. I drop to my knees as my sword sputters, then goes black, coated with ash. Once again energy spins around me, a bright whirlwind of fire. A dark-haired angel floats above me, his arms spread wide as the flame flows back into his chest, leaving a heart-shaped glow on his breast.

My vision is blotted by black spots as the light fades, but I swear the angel winks at me as he turns his thumb up in a gesture of approval. He grins and says, "Not bad, but a better song would have been 'Return to Sender.'"

"Noted," I say, barely able to hold my head up. My vision blurs and the angel is gone. The only thing above me is a tin roof. I cradle the dog to my breast as I stagger back to my feet, stumbling toward the open door. I need fresh air.

There's a splash near my feet as I make it outside. I look down. I'm standing in blood. I barely push my faceplate up before I start to vomit. As Sherry might say, I "puke my guts out." Only, literally. By the time I'm done, my intestines have slipped out of my wound and are wedged between my skin and breast plate. I hope that girder was sterile.

I finally gather my wits enough to wonder about the source of the blood. It's not all mine, is it? I look around and find a dead cultist a yard away. Nine other bodies lie scattered across the weed-covered parking lot.

There's a single car, headlights blazing, the motor idling. I inch toward it, spotting the dark-robed figure silhouetted beyond the lights, pistol in hand.

I stagger past the headlights. No longer blinded, I see who I thought I'd see.

Brother Anthony takes the Chihuahua from my rubbery arms.

"This was the vessel?" he asks, in a business-like tone.

I nod.

"We'll have Brother Berthold examine him. Perhaps his life can be spared."

"You can't tell because of the armor, but I'm bleeding to death," I whisper.

He places an arm around me and helps me into the car. It's a big Mercedes. Even in my armor, the back seat is roomy. I drape a steel clad forearm across my eyes as I collapse onto the soft leather.

"We're fortunate that it's Halloween," says Brother Anthony. "It may be the only night a monk can bring an armor clad woman to an emergency room without arousing undue curiosity."

"Way to see the silver lining," I say, or try to say; I have no idea if he understands my mumbles.

"Despite your injuries, this night has been a victory. We defeated the Golden Veil, and you dispatched Cerberus swiftly enough to avoid a large-scale escape. After the doctors mend you, you can recuperate at the monastery while we research any evil spirits that may have slipped loose."

I move my arm and open my eyes. I can see the stars pass overhead through the back window of the car. I feel a little stronger now that I'm on my back. What blood I have left is finding an easier path to my brain. I don't feel great, but I might be able to fight off slipping into a coma for another five minutes.

"I'm not going back to the monastery," I whisper.

He's quiet.

"I want to stay in school. I can heal in my dorm room."

"There's no point in attending this college. Your studies have taken you far past the level of anything the classes here have to offer."

"The stuff I need to learn isn't in books. I don't know how to talk to people. I don't know how to judge who to trust."

"You need only trust us."

"You said if a razor touched my skin I'd lose my strength, like Sampson. I shaved my legs and still yanked Cerberus around like a puppy."

There's a strange sound from the front seat.

"Are you grinding your teeth?"

"The biblical texts do not address whether Sampson shaved his legs," Brother Anthony admits.

I laugh, but quickly stop as my innards slosh.

"I drank coffee this week. I even tried a beer."

I can see the side of his head. The vein in his temple is bulging.

"Maybe it's not prayer and fasting that gives me my powers. Maybe they're just part of me. My father is an angel who thinks that earth has rewards that heaven can't offer. Perhaps wanting to have fun is just part of who I am."

"These are dangerous thoughts."

I close my eyes. Everything fun is dangerous. Perhaps I'm on a path angels should fear to travel. Treading down to the end of Lonely Street, straight on through the Heartbreak Hotel, out the back door, to whatever lies beyond. The angel spark that dwells within me won't be nurtured by prayer and meditation in some quiet, hidden valley. If I ever hope to blow the spark into a flame, I'll need the whirlwind of the wide, wild world.

Even an angel needs a little Elvis in her soul.

SECRET ORIGINS

Since I was raised in a fundamentalist household, there was a lot of stuff I missed out on in popular culture. We weren't supposed to go to movies, our television viewing was heavily regulated, and rock and roll was the devil's music. The church I went to practiced speaking in tongues and casting out of demons. Sometimes, men would get "possessed by the Holy Spirit" and run around the church on the backs of the pews.

So, I was an outsider because of religion. Then, I became an atheist, and became an outsider from that religion, and found myself stranded between worlds.

Crystal's inner struggles of trying to figure out where she belongs in a world she wasn't trained to deal with grow directly from my own turbulent late teens.

I suspect she'll figure it out. I know I did, eventually.

PENTACLE ON HIS FOREHEAD, LIZARD ON HIS BREATH

I RAN THREE red lights trying to reach David before the cops did. I steered with one hand and had the cell phone in the other, trying to talk him down. Five minutes had passed since David called me for help, whispering, sounding paranoid, which was good, paranoid was good. Paranoid might keep him cautious. With luck, he hadn't given anyone a reason to call 911. What worried me was that he'd stopped responding. I was pretty sure he'd dropped his phone. I kept yelling, "It's okay! I'm almost there!" but the only reply was distant shouting, something about keys. Or maybe monkeys.

I slowed to a less noticeable speed before reaching Adam's Art Supplies. I was relieved that only a few passers-by stared at David as he waved his arms and shouted at the open door of his van. Probably the cops weren't on their way, but I decided to assume they were. This scene was the worst nightmare of every friendly neighborhood drug dealer. Acid was developed as a truth serum. Who knew what David might tell the cops about me?

"David," I said as I got out of the car, two parking spaces behind him. He looked up, then down, and stopped shouting. He reached to the asphalt and picked up his cell phone.

"Buzz?" he asked into it.

I kept my voice calm and steady. "I'm right behind you, David. You don't need the phone."

"Okay," he said into the phone.

I switched from calm to condescending. "David, man, I'm disappointed. You know what I told you about set and setting."

He twisted his torso and neck around to look at me, as if his shoes were nailed to the ground. He stood in the middle of a messy smear of paint. He'd dropped his bag of art supplies and had been stepping on the tubes, bursting them. Muddy, flesh-toned sneaker prints showed evidence of his pointless meandering around the van.

"Buzz! Thank God you're here."

"How you doing, David?" I noticed that he'd drawn an upside-down pentacle on his forehead in ballpoint pen. "Looks like you might be having a little bit of a bad trip."

"No, no. I was doing fine until they took my keys."

"Who?" I asked, worried that some conscientious citizens had already tried to intervene.

"The monkeys."

"What monkeys, David?"

He rolled his eyes and pointed at the van. He stammered, plainly frustrated at explaining the obvious. "The *monkeys* in the *van*."

"I don't see any monkeys," I said. "It's okay. I think they've gone."

He ran his hand through his hair, leaving a wet red streak. I thought he was bleeding, until I realized it was paint. He stared at me, looking nervous. "No," he said, dropping his voice to a raspy whisper. "They're invisible monkeys."

I nodded. "Makes sense. I can't see them."

"They've taken my keys and locked the doors."

I looked into the open vehicle. The keys were in the ignition. I leaned in and grabbed them. He snatched my arm and yanked me back.

"Are you crazy?" he asked. "They crush skulls with those jaws. They eat brains, Buzz. It's their *Jello*. Don't you know anything?"

I pushed the van door shut with my free arm.

"It's okay," I said, jiggling the keys so he'd notice them. "They're trapped now."

David loosened his grip on my arm. I could see him trying to fit this turn of events into the fractured dream-story in his head. I carefully, cautiously placed my arms around him and hugged him. "It's okay," I whispered. "You're safe now."

Some people think pushers don't give a damn about their clients. But this is a business like any other, and the secret of any long-term relationship is customer service. I sold David the acid. I'd help get him down. David was my favorite customer. His money/sense ratio was heavily skewed toward money. He spent in a weekend what other clients spend in a year. It would break my heart to see him go to jail.

David swayed in my arms for several long seconds, then pushed me away, shaking his head.

"I'm cool," he said.

"You're cool?" I asked.

"Cool. It's cool."

I looked around. Everyone watching turned away. My appearance on the scene had released them from the potential responsibility of dealing with the psychotic screamer in their midst. They could now stay uninvolved without guilt. But the sooner we got out of the open, the better.

"Why don't I take you back to your place?" I said. "We can come back for the van later."

He nodded.

"Why'd you come out anyway? You know what I told you. It's set and setting. You've got to have the right mindset, and you've got to be in a place with positive energies. You definitely shouldn't be out driving around."

"Ran out of ghost juice," he said. "Decided to make a mayonnaise run."

I nodded, figuring it made sense to him, and wasn't important to me. I knelt down to gather up the scattered tubes. A large tube of white had somehow escaped trampling. David dropped to his knees. I winced at the sound of his kneecaps hitting the asphalt.

"My God," he said, staring at the smeared and swirled paints that coated the parking space. *"My God."*

"What?" I asked.

"Don't you see?" He opened his arms before him, encompassing the scene, a look of serenity over him.

"What?" I tried to control my impatience.

"It's him," he said, contemplating the muddy smear. "It's my father's face."

I rubbed my temples. *Of course.* David has this *thing* about his father.

Luckily, David fell quiet after that. I was able to guide him into my car. I noted the paint he was getting on the seats and floor mat. I would add the cleaning cost to his tab. He wouldn't mind. David had a nearly bottomless well of money from some kind of trust fund. As I closed my door I heard sirens, still a few blocks away. I drove off calmly, merging into traffic as a black and white pulled into the parking lot. No problem. Everything was good. No harm except for a little mess from spilled paints. The cops wouldn't waste time on this.

"Teakettle," David said.

I nodded in agreement. Occasionally, acid will make you pull the wrong words down from the little shelves in your head. No sense in trying to puzzle it out.

"We'll get you home in a jiffy," I said. "Get you to bed. You look tired."

"I haven't slept in three days."

"Really?" I asked, forgetting the question was useless.

"Three or seven." He held up four fingers. "The ecstasy keeps me boiling."

"Right." Whatever was keeping him going wasn't ecstasy, though, since the E he'd bought from me was just generic Sudafed.

Fortunately, David didn't live far, just down by the campus. He lived in the attic of this old Victorian house. The whole floor was his, a huge space, which he used as a studio for his paintings. David's stuff was pretty good, but he was nowhere as famous as his father. Of course, his father hadn't gotten famous until after he was dead. I guided David up the stairs. His body was trembling, his face pale and sweaty. The drugs were still riding him hard. But once I got him into his apartment, I could turn him over to his girlfriend Celia and be done with this.

Except, of course, Celia wasn't home. Or at least she wasn't answering the knocks. The only sound from inside was a steady, shrill whistle.

"Where's Celia, David?"

"Oh. She left. We had a fight."

"Too bad."

"She was trying to hide all the knives."

"Hmm," I said.

"So I had to do the ritual with a toenail clipper."

"Ah," I said.

Fortunately, I still had his keys, so getting in wasn't a problem.

The place was a mess. Books and canvases were scattered everywhere, and black plastic bags had been hung over the windows. Squat candles guttered at two points of a pentacle that had been laid out on the floor with duct tape. The other candles were extinguished, reduced to shapeless pools of wax. A horrible odor filled the air, like something burning. A cloud of steam rolled from the little curtained off area at the back of the studio that served as the kitchen.

"Teakettle," David said, moving toward the kitchen. He took the shrieking kettle off the tiny electric stove. He opened the top, and all but vanished in the steam cloud that issued forth. The stench gagged me.

"My herbalist recommended this lizard," he said. "Reconnect with the dinosaur within. Mainline to the oblongata." I assumed he was grabbing the wrong words again until I noticed a baggie of dried reptile parts on the counter, labeled with a Chinese script.

"Sure," I said, picking up the baggie, staring at the recognizable heads and eyes looking back at me. "*My* stuff is illegal. Jesus, David, you'll put anything in your mouth, won't you?"

"At least once," he said, pouring himself a cup of the tea, which trickled from the spout with the speed and thickness of jet black honey. "Want any?"

"Pass," I said. I headed away from the kitchen before he actually drank the stuff. I pride myself on a strong stomach, but hey. I looked at the canvases propped up around the room. This was stuff I hadn't seen before. David had abandoned his realistic style and was painting very dark shapes now, geometric, almost architectural, like shadowy rooms and halls, but off somehow, sinister.

As David relieved himself in the bathroom, I stooped to take a closer look at his reading material. There were a dozen books propped open on the floor. All his books were stained. The corners of LeVay's *Book of the Living* were smudged with mustard. Saint Germaine's *The Door Beyond Death* had been dropped into the tub at some point, and was now brown and warped. Crowley's *Magic and Mind* had paint-smeared pages ripped out and tacked against the legs of the easel. I got a closer look at the painting on the easel. From across the room, the canvas looked blank. Now, I could see it was glazed with brush-stroked mayonnaise that was starting to turn a little yellow.

Perched on a small table near the easel was the only pristine book in the room. It was a copy of *Into Madness*. I'd heard about it, of course. It was the book that had just been published about David's father, Alex Cambion. I skimmed over the excerpt on the back cover. Alex had been an illustrator for magazines in the seventies, before David was born. Some people said he painted like Norman Rockwell then, but that wasn't the work that made him famous.

David came out of the bathroom, naked.

"You going to stick around?" he asked.

"You still tripping?"

"How can I tell?" he asked. "Maybe. I've been asleep for three days now."

"Awake," I said.

"Whatever. I don't think the acid had any effect. I still feel too grounded."

"I think it had more effect than you might be noticing, man." I studied his face. It was hard to tell if he was fully back. Acid can be surprisingly subtle. Its effects can ebb and flow. "It was good stuff. I play straight with you."

He nodded. "You might be the only friend I have left, Buzz. Did you know Celia left me?"

"I heard."

"She thinks I'm crazy," he said, a sweep of his hand directing my gaze to the duct-tape pentacle. "I've been trying to talk to my father."

"Nothing crazy there," I said. "Lot's of people miss their folks when they pass on."

"I can't remember him," said David. "He killed himself when I was seven. He was schizophrenic. He'd been living in an asylum since I was five."

"Bad break," I said.

"Was it? Last week my grandmother auctioned one of Father's asylum paintings for nine million, and that's not a record for his work. His suffering has paid for everything I own."

"Huh," I said. "Kind of his gift to you, maybe."

"No," said David. "I've been trying to get inside his mind. I've been trying to get into his world with the drugs and the sleep and the rituals." He shook his head. "I've gotten on the edge, I think. I keep getting close. But I'm too *sane*. Father didn't know his own name at the end. Words were just a maze to him. All he understood by the end was how to put paint onto canvas. Some people say they find a language in his final paintings. I've never understood the vocabulary."

He seemed lucid now, as lucid as a sweaty naked man with a pentacle on his forehead and lizard on his breath is ever likely to be. I edged my way to the door. "You seem to be feeling better."

"Better is so relative," he said, bending over to place new candles at the points of the pentacle. "Ever since that book came out, I've just been so..."

After a moment, I realized he wasn't going to finish the sentence. He began to light the candles.

He stood in the middle of the pentacle, his eyes closed, his hands folded before him in a prayer, his paintbrush pointing toward heaven. The way he held his arms, I could see for the first time the deep scratches along the insides of his wrist.

Wonderful. No wonder Celia had hidden the knives. I decided to stick around until David fell asleep. If he'd really been awake three days, I wouldn't have to wait long. Acid and lizard tea couldn't keep a person going forever.

I snatched a beer from his fridge and plopped onto the couch. David was saying a prayer, mumbling most of the words. I tuned him out. A lot of addicts are into this mystic mumbo jumbo. They use the acid to try to "rend the veil of reality" as David put it. They're convinced that there's something more than their physical body and the world they can see with their eyes. I have no financial incentive to argue. But my years in the business have led me to one pretty solid conclusion: People are nothing but chemistry. There's no soul or spirit separate from our bodies. We're just big, walking pots of brain fluid soup. We can change the way we think and feel by adding the right spices, a little acid here, a little pot there, simmer in some beer, and hey, you get happy stew if you don't set the heat too high and get scorched. All the occult B.S., the prayers, the candles, were harmless, but pointless.

At last, David finished murmuring, opened his eyes, and focused on the canvas.

He said, "My grandmother says that the first real sign that something was wrong was when Dad began having problems with insomnia. Just after I was born. He was twenty-three. And now I'm twenty-three."

He dipped the brush into dark blue paint and began to work. I watched him for a while. I broke into a second beer, then a third. He seemed very calm. The way he painted was almost like a dance. His whole body swayed and dipped as his brush swirled across the canvas. Night fell and the little light that seeped around the trash bags dimmed. The candles cast strange shadows. On the walls, it was almost like two people stood before the canvas, moving independently, one slow and deliberate, the other manic. The air was stuffy and warm. At some point, I must have fallen asleep.

It was David who woke me.

"See what I have done," he said.

I looked at my watch. He'd been at this all night. I was stiff and dry-mouthed. Blearily, I allowed myself to be led to the canvas. My eyes popped open, wide-awake. I'd seen plenty of David's work. He was talented, sure, but this was something else. It was rendered with near photographic detail. It seemed like it should have taken days to paint. David must have worked like a demon to finish it in a single night. And from his twisted, drug-altered mind, had sprung... tranquility.

The painting was reminiscent of a *Saturday Evening Post* cover. A painter sat before his canvas, and his toddler son was in his lap. The painter looked down, beaming with pride, at his son with a brush in his hand and paint all over his clothes. And the canvas they sat before was like a mirror, with a boy and his father painting from the other side, and behind them sat a mirror, in which the larger painting was recreated, and within this was a canvas recreating the scene, and so on. The detail was amazing, but even more impressive were the expressions on the faces. There was so much happiness captured here. And yeah, corny as it sounds, even love.

"Whoa," I said. "This is really good. Really, really good. The faces... whoa."

"He doesn't remember this," said David. "My son was only two at the time. But he used to sit with me for hours. He loved to watch me work. He would fall asleep in my lap."

I sighed. He was still tripping. David didn't have kids.

"David," I said, "you're wearing me thin, man."

"He thinks you're his friend," said David. "You have to tell him something important for me. He'll believe you."

"Forget it," I said, rubbing my eyes. I was tired of this trip, tired of puzzling out drug logic. Would this weird mother never crash? "Write yourself a note or something. I'm going home."

David grabbed me by the shoulders and pulled us face to face. His grip was unbelievable, the kind of strength you get with PCP or something.

"Listen to me, punk," said David. "You know who I am. Don't play with me."

"I know who you think you are," I said, in the most soothing voice I could muster. "You're tripping. You're not Alex Cambion. Snap out of this."

"My time remaining is short. I would as soon spit on you as speak to you. You're a detestable poisoner of souls, but you're the only one within reach. I pray you have one tiny shred of decency within you."

"Dude," I said. "Chill out. I'm your friend. You know you can trust me."

"Then tell him," said David, his voice trembling on the edge of tears. "Tell him I loved him."

"Sure, no problem, I'll tell him. Trust me."

Finally, his eyes closed, and he collapsed in my arms. I dragged him to the couch. He felt light as a skeleton.

At last I was free to leave. I'd been around enough to know that a crash this hard wouldn't be over any time soon. He was out at least the next 12 hours, maybe more.

I went back to my life, happy that the worst of the ordeal was over. I swung back that night to check on him, expecting him to be zonked out, and found him awake. He was sitting on the floor in front of the canvas, his cheeks sunken, dark, heavy bags beneath his eyes.

"You okay?" I asked.

"This painting is still wet," he said, staring at his paint-covered fingertips.

"You painted it last night. No big surprise. Don't oils take a while to dry?"

"Oils need a lot of time to dry. It takes weeks to paint some things because of this. Even with a month I couldn't have painted this," said David. "I've never had his skill."

"You never know what you have in you," I said.

"It's signed by him. Alex Cambion."

"Huh," I said, looking at the signature. "Sorry dude, I was here. Watched you work on it. It's yours. Maybe that acid did you good. Better art through chemistry."

"It's like a message from him," said David, his voice cracking. "But I was never with him when he painted. This is like something to taunt me, something to remind me of a life I never had."

"Maybe you just didn't get close enough to understand him, man. You still need to do more inner work to touch the space he was in."

"Yeah," said David. "I guess so."

"Look, you tripped pretty hard these last few days. If you need it, I got some stuff that will help you sleep. You drink plenty of water, get some rest, and maybe in a week or so you'll be ready to try again."

"I don't know."

"It's worth a shot. I sold you Sunshine last time. But a shipment of Hearts is coming down next week. It's pricier, but should give you a little more control, and let you go deeper than your last trip. All you need is the right set and setting."

"Maybe," said David, scratching the scabs along his wrist, his voice distant and tired. "Maybe. I just want to connect with him, you know. I want to know if he even knew I was alive. That's all I'm asking. Just, maybe, if, you know, he loved me."

I nodded, then said, "David... maybe... next time you'll find out."

I talked a little longer to make sure he was okay. I left him only after I was sure he wasn't a danger to himself, and with the promise that he would get some sleep. As for what he'd said to me the night before, I guess David is brain-fried enough that he might believe that his father's ghost borrowed his body. But I know what's best. David is the sort who can take almost anything and twist it around until it tortures him. What kind of guy would I be if I didn't watch out for my best customer?

🟦🟦🟦🟦🟦🟦🟦🟦🟦🟦🟦🟦🟦🟦🟦

SECRET ORIGINS

I wrote this story at Orson Scott Card's Writing Boot Camp in 2000. We were supposed to go out and look for story ideas from events we spotted in the real world. As I was driving to a Mexican grocery store hoping to find inspiration there, I passed a guy standing next to a van yelling into the open door. When I drove past, I didn't see anyone inside the van. Instantly, I knew I'd found the seed for my story.

We only had one day to write. I went home and lit my tiki torches and sat on the deck until 5 a.m. banging out this story. The lizard tea is real stuff, by the way. One of my ex-wives believed in alternative medicines and her healer prescribed this. I never tasted it, but, man, to this day I remember the way it smelled, and can't forget all the loose scales at the bottom of the bag.

Card hated the story by the way. But, most of the other Boot Campers seemed to like it, and afterwards a few of the others students came up to talk to me about their own experience with acid. I will say, by the way, that I've never used the stuff, or any illegal drugs. The stuff happening in my skull is strange enough without assistance.

To Know All Things That Are
in the Earth

TO KNOW ALL THINGS THAT ARE IN THE EARTH

A LLEN FROST ASSUMED the first cherub was part of the restaurant's Valentine's decorations. He and Mary sat on the enclosed patio at Zorba's. He'd taken a pause to sip his wine when he first noticed the small angel behind the string of red foil hearts that hung in the window. The cherub was outside, looking like a baby doll with a pair of pasted-on wings.

A second cherub fluttered down, wings flapping. A third descended to join them, then a fourth. Allen thought it was a little late in the evening to still be putting up decorations, but he appreciated the work someone had put into the dolls. Their wings moved in a way that struck him as quite realistic, if realistic was a word that could be used to describe a flying baby.

Then the first cherub punched the window and the glass shattered. Everyone in the room started screaming. The cherubs darted into the restaurant, followed by a half dozen more swooping from the sky. Mary jumped up, her chair falling. Before it clattered against the tile floor, a cherub grabbed her arm. She shrieked, hitting it with her free hand, trying to knock it loose, until another cherub grabbed her by the wrist.

Allen lunged forward, grabbing one of the cherubs by the leg, trying to pull it free. He felt insane — the higher parts of his brain protested that this couldn't be happening. Nonetheless, his sensory, animal self knew what was real. His fingers were wrapped around the warm, soft skin of a baby's leg. White swan wings held the infant aloft. A ring of golden light the size of a coffee cup rim hovered above the angel's wispy locks. The whole room smelled of ozone and honeysuckle. The cherub's fat baby belly jiggled as Allen punched it.

The angel cast a disapproving gaze at Allen, its dark blue eyes looking right down to Allen's soul. Allen suddenly stopped struggling. He felt inexplicably naked and ashamed in the face of this creature. He averted his eyes, only to find himself staring at the angel's penis, the tiny organ simultaneously mundane, divine and rude. He still had a death grip on the cherub's leg. Gently, the cherub's stubby hands wrapped around Allen's middle and ring fingers. The cherub jerked Allen's fingers back with a *SNAP*, leaving his fingernails flat against the back of his wrist.

Allen fell to his knees in pain. Mary vanished behind a rush of angels, a flurry of wings white as the cotton in a bottle of aspirin. Her screams vanished beneath the flapping cacophony. Somewhere far in the distance, a trumpet sounded.

THE RAPTURE WAS badly timed for Allen Frost. He taught biology at the local community college while working on his doctorate. This semester, he had a girl in his class, Rachael Young, who wouldn't shut up about intelligent design. She monopolized his classroom time. Her endless string of leading questions were thinly disguised arguments trying to prove Darwin was crap. He'd been blowing off steam about Rachael when he'd said something really stupid, in retrospect.

"People who believe in intelligent design are mush-brained idiots," he said. "The whole idea of God—"

"I believe in God," Mary said.

"But, you know, not in *God* God," Allen explained. "You're open-minded. You're spiritual, but not religious."

Mary's eyes narrowed into little slits. "I have very strong beliefs. You just don't take them seriously."

Allen sighed. "Don't be like this," he said. "I'm only saying you're not a fundamentalist."

Mary still looked wounded.

Allen felt trapped. Most of the time, he and Mary enjoyed a good relationship. They agreed on so much. But when talk turned to religion, he felt, deep in his heart, they were doomed. Their most heartfelt beliefs could never be reconciled.

Allen lifted his wineglass to his lips and took a long sip, not so much to taste the wine as to shut up before he dug the hole any deeper. He turned his attention to the cherubs outside the window. Then his brains turned to mush.

Because, when you're wrestling an angel—its powerful wings beating the air, its dark, all-knowing eyes looking right through you—you can't help but notice evolution really doesn't explain such a creature. The most die-hard atheist must swallow his pride and admit the obvious. An angel is the product of design.

A YEAR AFTER the Rapture, Allen tossed his grandmother's living room furniture onto the lawn, then whitewashed the floor.

When he was done, Allen went out to the porch to read while the floor dried. It had been four hours, eleven minutes since he'd put his current book down. He'd grown addicted to reading, feeling as uncomfortable without a book in hand as a smoker without a cigarette. He purchased his reading material, and the occasional groceries, with income he made reading tarot cards; he was well known to his neighbors as a magician. He always informed his hopeful visitors he didn't know any real magic. They came anyway. The arcane symbols painted all over the house gave people certain ideas.

The books that lined the shelves of his library only added to his reputation for mysticism. He was forever studying some new system of magic—from voodoo to alchemy to cabala. Much of the global economy had collapsed after the Rapture, but supernatural literature experienced a boom.

He did most of his trading over the internet. The world, for the most part, was intact. It wasn't as if the angels came down and ripped out power lines or burned cities. They had simply dragged off God's chosen. No one was even certain how many people were gone—some said a billion, but the official UN estimate was a comically understated one hundred thousand. The real hit to the economy came in the aftermath of the rapture; a lot of people didn't show up for work the next day. Allen suspected he could have found a reason to do his job if he'd been a fireman or a cop or a doctor. But a biology teacher? There was no reason for him to get out of bed. He'd spent the day hugging Mary's pillow, wondering how he'd been so wrong. He spent the day after that reading her Bible.

He hadn't understood it. Even in the aftermath of the Rapture, it didn't make sense to him. So he'd begun reading books written to explain the symbolic language of the Bible, which later led him to study cabala, which set him on his quest to understand the world he lived in by understanding its underlying magical foundations.

Jobless, unable to pay his rent, he'd moved into his grandmother's abandoned house where he'd studied every book he could buy, trade or borrow to learn magic. So far, every book was crap. Alchemy, astrology, chaos magic, witchcraft—bullshit of the highest order. Yet, he kept reading. He tested the various theories, chanting spells, mixing potions, and divining tea leaves. He was hungry for answers. How did the world really work? Pre-rapture, science answered that question.

But science, quite bluntly, had been falsified. The army of

angels had carried away his understanding of the world.

Allen now lived in a universe unbounded by natural laws. He lived in a reality where everything was possible. Books were his only guide into this terra incognita.

THE WHITEWASH DRIED, leaving a blank sheet twenty feet across. It was pristine as angel wings. Allen crept carefully across it, having bathed his feet in rainwater. He wore pale, threadbare cotton. He'd shaved his head, even his eyebrows. The only dark things in the room were his eyes and the shaft of charcoal he carried. He crouched, recited the prayer he'd studied, then used his left hand to trace the outer arc of the summoning circle. The last rays of daylight faded from the window. His goal, before dawn, was to speak with an angel.

With the circle complete, he started scribing arcane glyphs around its edges. This part was nerve-wracking; a single misplaced stroke could ruin the spell. When the glyphs were done, Allen filled the ring with questions. Where was Mary? Would he see her again? Was there hope of reunion? These and a dozen other queries were marked in shaky, scrawled letters. His hand ached. His legs cramped from crouching. He pushed through the pain to craft graceful angelic script.

It was past midnight when he finished. He placed seven cones of incense along the edge of the circle and lit them. The air smelled like cheap after-shave.

He retrieved the polished sword from his bedroom and carried it into the circle, along with the *Manual of Solomon*. He opened to the bookmarked incantation and spoke the words. Almost immediately, a bright light approached the house. Shadows danced on the wall. A low, bass rumble rattled the windows.

A large truck with no muffler was clawing its way up the gravel driveway.

Disgusted by the interruption, Allen stepped outside the circle and went to the front porch, book and sword still in hand. The air was bracing—the kind of chill February night where every last bit of moisture has frozen out of the sky, leaving the stars crisp. The bright moon cast stark shadows over the couch, end-tables, and lamps cluttering the lawn.

Allen lived in the mountains of southern Virginia, miles from the nearest town. His remote location let him know all his neighbors—and the vehicle in his driveway didn't belong to any of them. It was a flatbed truck. Like many vehicles these days, it was heavily armed. A gunner sat on the back, manning a giant machinegun bolted to the truck bed. The fact that the gunner sat in a rocking chair took an edge from the menace a gun this large should have projected. Gear and luggage were stacked on the truck bed precariously. A giant, wolfish dog stood next to the gunner, its eyes golden in the moonlight.

The truck shuddered to a halt, the motor sputtering into silence. Loud bluegrass music seeped through the cab windows. It clicked off, and the passenger door opened. A woman got out, dressed in camouflage fatigues. She looked toward the porch, where Allen stood in shadows, then said, "Mr. Frost?"

Allen assumed they were asking about his grandfather. The mailbox down at the road still bore his name—his grandmother never changed it after he died, nor had Allen bothered with it after his grandmother had vanished.

"If you're looking for Nathan Frost, he died years ago."

"No," the woman said, in a vaguely familiar voice. "Allen Frost."

"Why do you want him? Who are you?"

"My name is Rachael Young," she answered.

The voice and face clicked. The intelligent design girl from his last class. "Oh," he said. "Yes. You've found me."

The driver's door opened and closed. A long-haired man with a white beard down to his waist came around the front of the truck. "Well now," the old man said, in a thick Kentucky accent. "You're the famous science fella."

"Famous?" asked Allen.

"My granddaughter's been talking you up for nigh on a year," said Old Man Young. "Says you're gonna have answers."

"We looked all over for you," said Rachael. "The college said you'd gone to live with your grandmother in Texas."

"Texas? I don't have any relatives in Texas."

"No shit," the gunner on the flatbed said. "Been all over this damn country, chasin' one wild goose after another. You better not be a waste of our time." The dog beside him began to snarl as it studied Allen.

"Luke," said Old Man Young. "Mind your language. Haul down the ice-chest."

"Sorry we got here so late, Mr. Frost," Rachael said, walking toward him. She was looking at the sword and book. "Have we, uh, interrupted something?"

"Maybe," Allen said. "Look, I'm a little confused. Why, exactly, have you been looking for me?"

"You're the only scientist I trust," she said. "When we used to have our conversations in class, you always impressed me. I really respected you. You knew your stuff. Since your specialty is biology, we want you to look at what we've got in the cooler and tell us what it is."

Allen wasn't sure what struck him as harder to swallow — that she'd spent a year tracking him down, or that she remembered the tedious cross-examinations she'd subjected him to as conversations.

Luke, the gunner, hopped off the truck carrying a large green Coleman cooler. It made sloshing noises as he lugged it to the porch. Luke was middle-aged, heavyset, crew cut. Rachael's father?

Luke placed the container at Rachael's feet. Rachael leaned over and unsnapped the clasp. "Get ready for a smell," she said, lifting the lid.

Strong alcohol fumes washed over the porch. Allen's eyes watered. The fumes carried strange undertones — corn soaked in battery acid, plus a touch of rotten teeth, mixed with a not-unpleasant trace of cedar.

"We popped this thing into Uncle Luke's moonshine to preserve it," Rachael said.

Despite the moonlight, it was too dark for Allen to make out what he was looking at. Rachael stepped back, removing her shadow from the contents. Allen was horrified to find these crazy people had brought him the corpse of a baby with a gunshot wound to its face. The top of its head was missing. The baby was naked, bleached pale by the brew in which it floated. There was something under it, paler still, like a blanket. Only, as his eyes adjusted, Allen realized the baby wasn't sharing the cooler with a blanket, but with some kind of bird—he could make out the feathers.

When he finally understood what he was looking at, his hands shook so hard he dropped his sword, and just missed losing a toe.

ALLEN LIT THE oil lamps while Luke lugged the cooler into the kitchen. Allen only had a few hours worth of gasoline left for the generator; he wanted to save every last drop until he was ready to examine the dead cherub. While Luke sat the corpse in the sink to let the alcohol drain off, Allen gathered up all the tools he thought he might need—knives, kitchen sheers, rubber gloves, Tupperware. Rachael was outside, taking care of the dog, and Old Man Young was off, in his words, "to secure the perimeter."

"That means he's gone to pee," Rachael had explained once her grandfather was out of earshot.

To take notes during the autopsy, Allen found a black Sharpie and a loose-leaf notebook half filled with notes he'd made learning ancient Greek. As he flipped to a blank page, he said, "I can't believe you shot one of these. I thought they were invulnerable. I saw video where a cop emptied his pistol into one. The bullets bounced off."

"Invulnerable?" Luke asked. "Like Superman?"

"Sure. Bulletproof."

"You think a brick wall is invulnerable?" Luke asked.

"Is this a rhetorical question?"

"Suppose you took a tack hammer to brick wall," Luke said. "Would it be invulnerable?"

"Close to it," said Allen.

"How about a sledgehammer?" asked Luke.

"Then, no, of course not."

"A cop's pistol is a tack hammer," said Luke, as he freed the rifle slung over his shoulder. "This is a sledgehammer. .50-caliber. Single shot, but one is all I need. This thing will punch a hole through a cast iron skillet."

He nodded toward the cherub draining in the sink. "This pickled punk never stood a chance."

"Not a particularly reverent man, are you Luke?" said Allen. "That's pretty harsh language to be calling an angel."

The back door to the kitchen opened and Rachael came in, followed by Old Man Young.

"Whatever the hell this is," said Luke, "it ain't no damn angel."

"It looks like an angel," said Allen. "I got up close to one during the Rapture."

"Shut your fool mouth!" snapped Old Man Young. To punctuate his sentence, he spat on the floor. "*Rapture.* Rachael, I thought this fella was smart."

"He *is* smart," said Rachael.

"He's a mush-brained idiot if he thinks the Rapture has happened," Old Man Young said.

Allen was confused. "You think it hasn't?"

"I'm still here, ain't I?" Old Man Young said. "I've been washed in the blood of the lamb, boy. I'm born again! When the Rapture comes, I'm gonna be borne away!"

Allen cast a glance at the sink. "Maybe Luke shot your ride."

"Naw," said Luke. "I was at the Happy Mart when this little monster started dragging off some Hindu guy. I ran to the truck and got Lucille." Luke patted the rifle. "Saved that

125

fella a fate worse than death."

"But—" said Allen.

"But nothing!" Old Man Young said. "Second Samuel, 14:20, says that it is the wisdom of angels to know all things that are in the earth!"

"A real angel would have known to duck," said Luke.

"And it wasn't the Rapture," said Rachael. "The creatures took people at random. Yeah, they grabbed some self-proclaimed Christians. But they also took Hindus, Buddhists, Muslims, Jews, and Scientologists. They took Tom Cruise right in the middle of shooting a film."

"Yeah," said Allen. "I saw that."

"Heaven ain't open to his kind," said Old Man Young.

"So how do you explain what happened?" asked Allen.

"Demons," said Old Man Young.

"Aliens, maybe," said Rachael.

"Government black ops," said Luke.

Allen had heard these theories before, and a dozen others. The Young's weren't the first people to disbelieve the Rapture. None of the alternative explanations made sense. Genetic manipulation gone awry, mass psychosis, a quantum bleed into an alternate reality—all required paranoid pretzel logic to work. He was still scientist enough to employ Occam's Razor, cutting away all the distracting theories to arrive at the simplest conclusion: God did it.

"I admit, what happened doesn't match popular ideas of the Rapture," Allen said. "I've studied Revelation in the original Greek, and can't make everything line up. I'm no longer convinced any ancient text has a complete answer. But I get little glimpses of insight from different sources. Maybe God used to try to communicate with Mankind directly. Maybe he spoke as clearly as possible, in God language, but people weren't up to the task of understanding him. They all came away with these little shards of truth; no one got the big picture."

"Son, I'm up to the task of understanding," said Old Man

Young. "The good ol' King James spells out everything. If you don't understand, you don't want to understand."

"If you think it was the Rapture," asked Rachael, "why would God have been so random? He took rich and poor, young and old, the kind and the wicked. It makes no sense."

"To us," said Allen. "But when I was a senior at State, I helped out on this big study involving mice. We did some blood work, identified mice with the required genes, then separated them from the general population and took them to a different lab. I wonder if the mice left behind sat around wondering why they weren't chosen. They would never understand our reasons."

"That's your theory?" asked Rachael. "We're lab mice?"

"No. But maybe the gap between our intellect and God's mind is larger than the gap between mice and men. Our inability to understand His selection criteria doesn't mean He acted at random."

"Son, you're proving what I always say," said Old Man Young. "Thinking too much makes you stupid."

Allen nodded. "Thinking too much hasn't made me any wiser or happier."

"Don't pay attention to Grandpa," said Rachael. "We need a thinker. We need someone who can study this body and tell us what it is."

"Why didn't you take it to the cops?" asked Allen.

"If the government knew we had this, we'd already be dead," Luke said.

Rachael frowned. "I think we might be endangering the world by not showing this to the government. Not that there's much government left."

"Which is more proof it weren't the Rapture," said Old Man Young. "No Antichrist."

Which was true. America had been through eight presidents in the last year. Anyone displaying even modest leadership skills quickly became a target of the legions of Antichrist stalkers roaming the capitals of the world. What was left of day to day civilization was staggering on more due to momentum than competent leadership.

"This is what the Illuminati want," said Luke. "Chaos. When they seize power, people will kiss their asses with gratitude."

"Since Uncle Luke shot it, he gets to decide who sees it," said Rachael. "Also, it's his cooler."

"I'm not the trusting sort," Luke said. "But Rachael says you're a good guy, and smart."

Allen rubbed his temples. "You think I'll know the difference between an alien, a demon, or a black-ops sci-fi construct?"

All three Youngs looked at him hopefully.

"Okay," he said. "I'll go power up the generator."

"I'll come with you," said Rachael. "Jeremiah's stalking around out there and you don't want to run into him alone."

"Jeremiah?"

"Our dog," said Luke. "He's killed more men than I have."

For a second, Allen considered whether the oil lanterns might not provide enough light after all. Then, he clenched his jaw and headed for the back door. If you're going to cut open an angel, you may as well do the job right.

The corpse looked slightly yellow under electric light. Allen weighed the angel on his bathroom scale and found it barely topped ten pounds. Aerodynamics weren't his specialty, but the cherub's wings seemed slightly more plausible. Swan-sized wings could support a swan, after all, and they weighed more than ten pounds.

Allen started his exam in the obvious place—the hollow bowl of the skull. He'd never dissected a human before, but what was left of the cranium looked normal. It was bone. He recognized bone. Somehow, he'd expected angels to be crafted of material more grand.

His first real clue he was well outside the realm of known biology was when he took a close look at the torn skin peeling away from the skull. He found a visible, subcutaneous layer of something that shouldn't have been there, on a human body at least. It was a thin, fibrous material, like cloth. He tugged on a frayed thread carefully with his tweezers. He couldn't pull a strand of the tightly knit material free. He could see, though, that it was porous — blood vessels and nerve fibers ran through it. Whatever this was, it had grown under the skin, rather than being implanted.

"I've never seen anything like this."

"I've eyeballed it up close," said Luke. "It looks like Kevlar. Sort of."

"Score one for black-ops," said Allen, pausing to jot a few notes.

"Aliens could use Kevlar too," said Rachael. "Stuff better than Kevlar."

Allen moved on to the wings. After twelve months soaking in moonshine, they had a dull, grayish tone to them. It wasn't difficult to pull a feather free. Without the body on the butcher's block, he would have supposed he was looking at a seagull feather. Intuitively, this made sense. If God had designed feathers as the perfect tool of flight, why not use the same blueprint for both angel and bird?

But flight wasn't simply a matter of having feathers, as any chicken could attest. A cherub's chest didn't have the depth to support the muscles to power these wings, did it?

He flipped the cherub over and felt its breasts. The muscles under the soggy skin were rock hard. He noted the cherub had nipples and a belly button. Was God simply fond of this look? Or was there a cycle of life in Heaven? Angel fetuses developing in angel wombs, angel babes suckling at the breasts of angel mothers?

He tried to cut open the cherub's chest. It proved impervious to the butcher knife.

"Try this," Luke said, handing him a folded knife. Allen flipped the knife open to reveal a ceramic blade, black as onyx and razor sharp.

"Fancy," said Allen. He tried it against the skin. The knife's edge scraped away the surface easily, but the subcutaneous material thwarted further advance. Whatever it was, it couldn't be pierced.

Not willing to give up, Allen tried a different approach. He peeled back the torn flesh of the skull and slipped the knife along the edge of the fibrous layer. To his delight, the torn edge yielded to the knife as he applied steady, firm pressure. Slowly, he worked the knife forward, peeling the flesh from the cherub's face, working his way down the throat. He discovered cherubs had tracheas and jugular veins. He confirmed they had collarbones. After a long, tedious operation, slicing the flesh a millimeter at a time, he peeled the angel's skin back from its torso and found ... muscle. Bones. Fatty deposits.

Ordinary matter.

He stepped back from the table and stretched his neck. He'd been bent over the cherub a long time; his muscles were stiff.

"Want some water?" Rachael asked, breaking the silence.

"No, thank you," Allen said, staring at the flayed thing before him. It was a relief, in a way, to know what his nightmares would be for the rest of his life. An angel opened, peeled like the fetal pigs he'd taken apart in freshman biology. He had taken something divine, an occupant of Heaven, and treated it with all the respect he might show a frog in formaldehyde.

If he wasn't damned before, he certainly was now.

And yet... and yet he couldn't turn back. Blasphemous as it was, he was going to keep cutting. His need for knowledge overrode his fear of offending the divine. Who knew what his next cut might reveal?

The muscle of the chest looked like meat, but was dense and unyielding, even to the ceramic knife. He managed to scrape off several strands of the tough muscle fibers — he would have traded every book in the house for a microscope at that moment.

He tried the stomach. The muscle here was also impervious, but a thin gap of ligament beneath the ribs showed good results when he sawed at it with the knife. In less than five minutes, he'd cut a hole into the chest cavity.

He leaned over to peer inside, seeing nothing but gray, bleached tissue — the angel's lungs? Of course, if it had a trachea, it would have lungs. As near as he could tell, with the exception of the bulletproof skin and dense muscles, the cherub was constructed like other animals. It had breathed air. It had fed its muscles with a complex network of arteries and veins. It commanded its body with a nervous system. What did this mean?

In frustration, completely ignoring any rational, measured approach, he dug his fingers into the cherub's chest and began to feel around. His fingers sent indecipherable signals as they pushed against objects both slimy and leathery, both hard and yielding. Was this the liver? His hand was buried to the wrist. These had to be intestines. This hard thing... a kidney? Feces in the gut? Clear fluid suddenly gushed from the penis. He'd found the bladder.

He turned his hand up, in search of the heart. Where the heart should have been, he found an egg.

At least, it felt like an egg, smooth, oval, hard, of a size that might earn it a Grade A Large. He wriggled his fingers around it, trying to get a better understanding. The angel gurgled as his efforts freed some last teaspoon of air from the lungs.

And then, with a *POP*, the egg came free. He closed his fingers and pulled it out with a sloppy, wet, farting sound.

His hand was covered with gray goop.

He opened his fingers to reveal something beautiful.

An ovoid object, gleaming yellow in the lamplight.

A golden egg.

Allen placed it in the Tupperware as everyone came over

for a closer look.

"Told you," said Luke. "It's a cyborg. This is the power source."

"It's alien technology," Rachael said.

"The devil's handiwork," said Old Man Young.

Allen didn't know. Allen felt completely empty of opinion, thought, or emotion. Confronted with something so far beyond his understanding, he felt unreal. The egg, he'd held it, he could see it, it was reality. He must be the thing out of place.

Then, to compound his sense of unreality, the egg moved on its own power, rocking lengthwise, coming to rest upright on its small end, seeming, almost, to hover.

The lights flickered. Allen's skin tingled as the air began to smell of rain.

"What's happening?" Rachael asked.

The lights went out.

There was a terrible hush. No one breathed. Slowly, Allen's eyes adjusted to the dim starlight seeping through the window. The faces of his guests were pale and ghostlike.

At last, Rachael whispered, "I don't hear the generator."

Allen breathed. Right. The generator. "It must have run out of gas," he said. "I thought I had enough for a couple of hours."

"It's been a couple of hours," said Luke. "You needed more gas, you shoulda said something. I got a five gallon can in back of the truck."

"I'll help you get it," said Old Man Young.

"I'll come too. I need some fresh air," Rachael said.

Allen didn't know if the Young's were trying to ditch him, but he wasn't going to play along if they were. He didn't want to be alone in the kitchen with... with whatever the golden egg was.

They went out to the front yard. He waited with Rachael on the porch while Luke and the grandfather walked down to the truck.

He could tell she wanted him to say something. She wanted him to say there was nothing to be afraid of.

He couldn't bring himself to speak the words.

The moon was low on the horizon; fingers of shadow grasped the yard. The still air carried the footsteps of the men walking across the gravel. The winter night was silent otherwise. Except... except, from a distance, a soft beat, like a muffled drum being struck. Then another, somewhat louder, then louder still when it repeated an instant later. A shadow grew across the yard and Allen understood he was listening to angel wings.

Luke heard them too. He looked up, freeing the big rifle from his shoulder. He was looking at something Allen couldn't see, something hidden by the roof of the porch. The first angel floated into view, descending as gracefully as an owl coming to rest on a branch. This was nothing like the cherubs. This was an adult-sized angel on wings the size of a small plane. The angel's body was covered in silver armor, but enough of the face showed through the helmet that Allen judged the angel to be female. The sword by her side showed she had come for war.

Luke fired. The bullet smacked into the angel's breastplate. She didn't flinch, continuing her descent to earth, landing mere feet in front of Luke, who was hastily reloading. With a casual gesture, the angel extended her arm, catching Luke in the chest and throwing him backward, far past the end of the truck. Luke landed limp and didn't move.

With a sudden flap of wings, a second angel swooped down, kicking Old Man Young as he scrambled onto the truck bed, perhaps going for the mounted gun.

Allen grabbed Rachael by the arm and pushed her toward the door to the living room.

"The circle!" he said. "Get into it!"

He stooped to retrieve his sword and the *Manual of Solomon* from where he'd left them on the porch. He heard the angel wings behind him, beating once, twice. The light faded as the shadows cast by the angel's wings approached. Not daring to look back, Allen dashed through the door, leaping for the circle. He was relieved to find Rachael had placed herself inside the protective drawing without smudging the edges. Then he realized she was still moving; she had wound up in the circle purely by accident.

"Stop!" he yelled, and to his relief, she froze. "We're safe here. They can't touch us!"

"Are you sure?" she said, spinning around, looking panicked.

"No," said Allen. "But if we're not safe here, where can we run?"

He turned to face the doorway, and found it filled with the bright form of the angel. The angel walked calmly toward the circle, her eyes fixed on Allen. She approached to arm's length before stopping. Rachael clung tightly to Allen's arm, digging her nails into his biceps. Allen gripped the sword tightly, then thrust it forward and said, "I... I command you in the name of — "

The angel smirked, and swatted the tip of the sword with her gauntlet-clad hand. The force of the blow twisted the weapon from Allen's grasp, sending it clattering across the floor.

"You have no idea what you are doing," the angel said, walking around the circle, studying the symbols. Her voice was deep and operatic, heavenly. "You've copied this without understanding it."

"Yes," said Allen, seeing no advantage in lying.

The angel completed her orbit of the circle, nodding appreciatively. She asked, "If a shaman from deep in the jungle were to be transported to a modern city, would he think of writing as magic? He would have no idea what the letters spelling 'KEEP OUT' might mean, only that people respected them, and stayed away. He might even learn to copy the strange symbols. Tell me: would that be magic?"

"If it isn't magic," Allen said, "I think you would already

have killed us."

As he spoke, there was a distant sound of barking.

"Jeremiah!" said Rachael. "They'll kill him!"

Glancing back to the door, Allen saw the second angel stepping onto the porch. She had Old Man Young draped across her shoulder, and was dragging Luke by the collar. The barking grew closer by the second.

The second angel stepped through the door, tossing her limp passengers roughly into the corner. Allen saw Jeremiah round the truck and turn at a sharp angle, skidding in the gravel before bolting toward the house.

The angel closed the door with seconds to spare. Jeremiah collided with a *THUMP*. A brief instant of silence followed before the dog resumed his frantic barking, clawing at the door.

The first angel said to the second, "Get the body."

The second angel nodded and vanished into the kitchen.

The remaining angel drew her sword. The weapon burst into flame. Allen cringed from the heat, holding on to Rachael to keep her from leaving the circle.

"Let us pretend I can't enter your little drawing," the angel said. "Does that make you feel safe?"

"No," said Allen. "I haven't felt safe for a long time. I've been frightened. I've been lost. I want... I need answers."

"Answers?" said the angel. "You're drowning in answers. Every molecule of your body vibrates with answers. You don't lack answers. You lack the wisdom to recognize them. Tonight, you've cut open an angel. You've held its soul in your hands. What did you learn?"

"I don't know," said Allen.

"You have a few more minutes to think it over," said the angel, moving toward the interior wall. "Before the smoke kills you." With a solid thrust, the angel pushed her flaming sword through the wall. On the other side there was a bookcase. Allen heard books and papers crash to the floor. Instantly, the air smelled of smoke. Allen clenched his fists, wanting to run and pull the sword free, but fear nailed his feet to the floor.

The room took on an eerie hush. Old Man Young groaned in his unconsciousness. Rachael began to sob.

Allen noticed Jeremiah had stopped barking.

The living room window exploded inward, shards of glass flying, as a gray snarling streak of fur and teeth smashed through. The angel turned, quickly, fluidly, and a second too slow. Jeremiah buried his teeth into the angel's left wing at its junction with the back, an area free of armor.

The angel gasped, stumbling in pain, trying to knock Jeremiah free. Allen held his ground in the circle, reaching back to grab Rachael's hand.

Rachael wasn't there. The door to the living room slammed against the wall as she dashed down the porch steps.

Allen watched the fight between dog and angel. The angel reached back, grabbing Jeremiah by a hind leg, tugging. The angel's face twisted in terrible pain. Jeremiah hung on as long as he could, snarling, struggling, but the angel was too strong. Allen winced at the sound of bones cracking. Jeremiah yelped as the angel yanked him free. The angel spun, swinging the dog in an arc. Allen ducked to avoid being knocked over. Then, by accident or design, the angel released Jeremiah in mid-swing and the dog sailed cleanly out the broken window.

By then Rachael was once again beside Allen, aiming the .50-caliber rifle.

"Nobody hurts my dog," she said, and fired. It was like lightning struck the room. The shot knocked Rachael off her feet, and left Allen with ringing ears and spots before his eyes.

A bright red circle appeared on the wall behind the angel's neck. The bare, armorless area just below her chin was dark and wet. The angel's eyes closed as she fell to her knees and sat there, slumped against the wall, her head drooped at an unnatural angle, her arms limp and lifeless by her side.

The room was filling with smoke. The second angel came back from the kitchen. Rachael fumbled with the bolt of the rifle, her hands trembling.

The second angel grabbed the body of the first, pulled the flaming sword from the wall and moved back into the kitchen. Allen heard the back door open. By now, the smoke was blinding.

Rachael slipped the new round into the chamber and closed it with a satisfying clack. "Ready," she said.

"I think... I think you chased them off," Allen said.

"I'm willing to take that chance," she said.

"Get outside. Watch the skies. I'll get your grandfather and your uncle."

By now, Old Man Young was coughing, and his eyes fluttered open. He whispered, "I heard... I heard Jeremiah. Is he okay?"

"Come on," Allen said, helping him rise. "The house is on fire!"

"Weren't we outside?" he asked, sounding only half-awake.

"Follow me," Allen said, dragging Luke toward the open door. To his relief, Old Man Young obeyed. Soon, Allen had dragged Luke down the front steps, down to the truck, where Rachael now manned the machinegun. Luke's breathing was ragged, but Allen didn't know how to help him. The main thing he knew about first aid was not to move a person who might have internal injuries, and he'd just dragged Luke fifty feet.

Allen scanned the skies. Bright white sparks flew into the night as flames nibbled through the roof. It wouldn't be long before the house was gone, taking his collected books, his months of notes and sweat and theories, to say nothing of his family history.

He took a deep breath and ran back inside.

The living room was oven hot. There wasn't much in here

to burn, though—just the floorboards and the wall studs. It was lucky he'd stripped the room down to drywall. He pushed forward, trying to reach the library, but it was no use. The heat from the open door was unbearable. The hair on his arms began to singe.

Allen stepped back, then staggered toward the kitchen. The back door stood open. Burning wallpaper lit the room a flickering red. Dark smoke rolled along the ceiling. He could see the butcher's block, now empty. The golden egg was gone.

Allen crouched, searching for fresher air. He noticed the wet red spot on the wall next to him. Angel blood.

Walls appear solid and impervious through most of daily life. In reality, most drywall is only an adult male fist and a surge of adrenaline away from having a good-sized hole knocked through it. Allen punched that hole, then a second, then a third. His knuckles were bleeding. He grabbed the edges of the punctured drywall, grunting as he tried to break free the section splattered with angel blood. The drywall wasn't on fire, but it was crazy hot. Allen wouldn't let go. He tugged with all his strength but the nails held tight. The wall was winning. In frustration, he screamed—a primal, animal howl of rage and pain, a sound that frightened him.

With a crack, the drywall twisted free. Allen stumbled outside clutching a three-foot chunk of the stuff to his chest.

Allen sat on the frozen ground as the house behind him roared into the night sky. He was dimly aware that Luke was awake now, sitting next to the trunk, drinking something from a thermos. He was also distantly conscious of something walking toward him, limping, panting, smelling like dog.

It *was* a dog. Jeremiah sat beside Allen. Allen looked into the dog's eyes. They were full of emotions, far more recognizable than what he'd seen in the eyes of the angel. Jeremiah was in obvious pain. Yet, Jeremiah looked concerned, as if worried about Allen's health. What's more, the dog had a cocky tilt to his head, and angel pinfeathers stuck between his teeth, which combined into reassuring vow of, "I've got your back."

Allen had angel blood all over his hands and chest. Or maybe it was his own blood after punching through the wall. He couldn't tell where his blood ended and the angel's began.

Blood. He'd expected angels to be full of divine secrets, to be filled with miraculous matter. Tonight he'd seen a hint of this, of things beyond his understanding. But, he'd seen far more things he'd understood intimately as a biologist—muscle and bone and blood.

Every molecule of his body vibrated with answers. Did he have the wisdom to understand them?

Jeremiah left his side to greet Rachael, who was approaching. "You okay?" she asked.

"I think so," said Allen.

"I guess it's still an open question," she said. "Whether those were aliens, I mean."

"I don't think so," said Allen.

"Black ops?"

"No," said Allen. "I think they were angels. I think they were created by God."

"Oh," said Rachael.

"I thought they would be full of divine material," said Allen raising his bloody hands. "Of strange and wondrous stuff. And what if they were?"

"What do you mean?"

"What if they *were* made of divine material? What if we all are? You, me, Jeremiah. The ground under us, the sky above... what if what we think of as ordinary matter is actually the building blocks of the divine? The laws of biology, of physics, of chemistry—these are the rules God follows. These are the ways He works His will. Science turns out to be the study of His divine mechanics."

As he said the words, he believed them. He didn't know if it was deduction, intuition, or simply faith, but he felt a powerful calm settle over him. He would probably never know the "why" of God. Why the Rapture? Why take Mary? Why create angels and men and dogs? Why the world? But the how—the how was knowable. Before the detour of this past year, he'd learned with some detail the "how." He'd thought that angels falsified science. But, studying the angel blood on the drywall on the grass, he understood, in their ordinary matter, angels confirmed science as the path to understanding the mind of God.

"Uncle Luke thinks he's broken a couple of ribs," said Rachael, apparently not knowing how to respond to his little epiphany.

"There's a hospital in Roanoke," said Allen. "We can be there in an hour."

He stood up and carried the chunk of drywall carefully, hoping not to contaminate it more than it already was. The next step in understanding the angels was beyond Allen's expertise. But part of the fun of being a scientist was talking to people who knew a lot more than you did about their specialties. In retrospect, he'd botched the autopsy of the angel, big time. If he'd gone to experts, asked for help, who knows what they could have learned? At least he had a shot at redeeming himself. You can collect a lot of DNA from a blood-spattered chunk of drywall.

He walked toward the truck, Jeremiah limping beside him. Allen knew a vet down the road. Hopefully Luke could survive a detour to drop off Jeremiah. In the battle between man and angel, the dog had made his loyalties clear, and deserved whatever care could be provided.

Old Man Young already had the truck revved up. It was decided that Luke and Jeremiah would ride in the cab due to their injuries. Allen and Rachael would have to ride on the back. Rachael abandoned the rocking chair and pressed up next to Allen against the cab as the truck began to pitch and sway down the driveway. From the jumbled mounds of gear, she produced a heavy quilt and pulled it over them.

It was disturbingly intimate, to be sharing a blanket with a woman with whom he'd shared such an adventure. He'd not thought about women at all since Mary was taken. He had a lot on his mind, as he watched his house burn, filling the heavens with a plume of sparks and smoke. He was, in the front of his mind, still trying to figure out what the night's events meant. But something in the back of his mind was more concerned with whether or not he should put his arm around Rachel, who was leaning her head on his shoulder.

Rachael, her voice soft and caring said, "I'm sorry about your house."

Allen shrugged. It was what it was. He knew, deep in his gut, that the chapter of his life the house represented was over. The house for him represented magical thinking — the notion that there were things that could happen outside the laws of science. He was almost glad to be rid of it.

"Things will be alright," he said. To his own ears, his voice was tired and thin, battered by stress and smoke. His lungs felt sandpapered, and his hands were starting to blister. To show that he meant the reassuring words, he put his arm around Rachael, and drew her closer. It felt right. More importantly, the world felt right. The night had brought him a newfound faith in the essential sensibleness of the universe.

"Can I ask you a question?" Rachael said, her face inches from his.

"Sure."

"Why did you have that circle drawn on your floor?"

Allen rolled his eyes. "It'll sound stupid."

"What?"

"I was trying to summon an angel."

"Guess it worked," said Rachael.

Allen's mouth went dry. Rachael's arrival with the cherub

had just been a coincidence, hadn't it? Old Man Young turned the truck onto the road and gunned the engine. Allen pulled the quilt tighter around them, to fend off the chill night air.

SECRET ORIGINS

For an atheist, I sure write a lot of stories about God and angels. What can I say? I was raised as a fundamentalist Christian. Bible mythology is in my blood. For what it's worth, Allen's grandmother's house in this story is laid out in my head exactly like my own grandmother's house.

This story was also written following my girlfriend's death from cancer. That summer, I went to a Bodies exhibit, one of the traveling shows where they've preserved actual cadavers and displayed them for people to gawk at, ostensibly for educational purposes. The thing was, I feel like I did get an education, because they had a cross section of a cancer-ridden lung. I had always thought of cancer as something separate, an invader, but seeing it first hand helped me realize that the cancer had been part of her, not an invasive disease, but the body itself getting its instructions ever so slightly wrong in a way that leads to disaster.

When you lose a loved one, you spend a lot of time asking yourself why. But, maybe there is no why. It's all just random; if one thing doesn't kill you, something else will, and there's no real meaning in how you go. In the absence of knowing why, perhaps we have to satisfy ourselves with knowing how. How is a question within the human capacity to answer.

Echo of the Eye

ECHO OF THE EYE
ରେଠ୯୪ଓ୫ରୀ

*K*IDD PUMPED QUARTER *after quarter into the washer at the Laundromat. The humid air was thick with the smell of bleach and Tide. The water in the window of the machine began to churn pink. A career as a butcher had left Kidd unusually skilled at removing blood stains.*

IT WAS AFTER MIDNIGHT when Jason pulled the RV into Hog Station, NC. This wasn't Jason's first trip to this tiny speck on the map. He'd visited two years ago when his father dumped Cassie at Stanley University, the ultra-conservative, unaccredited college that was the town's second claim to fame. As her father had pushed her out of the car into the arms of a pair of burley *advisors* she'd screamed at Jason, "When I get home I'll cut off your dick, traitor!" At least she'd been speaking to him. Cassie had been in a seven-year sulk since their mother died.

Jason returned to pick her up a year later, when their father passed. She'd ridden home with her eyes firmly fixed out the window and her lips tightly sealed. After the funeral she'd announced she wanted to go back to Hog Station. When he asked her why, she answered, "I like the barbecue."

At the time, he assumed Cassie had outgrown her vegetarian phase. When Jason dropped her off in front of her dorm, she'd said, "I'm sorry I threatened you." Not knowing what to say, he'd laughed uncomfortably and drove away, never guessing it would be the last time he'd see her alive.

Hog Station hadn't changed. Main Street was a row of brick shops facing a rusted railroad track. Most of the buildings were boarded up, with only a barber, a barrister, and a butcher still in business. Yet almost all the parking spaces were filled, not something Jason had expected to see at midnight. The roof of the butcher shop flickered with reddish light, as if on fire. Jason pulled the RV to the curb and opened his door. Smoke washed into his vehicle— savory, mouth-watering smoke. The sound of laughter rolled down from above.

Jason walked to the butcher shop door. Kidd's Meats, established 1879. This was Hogg Station's first claim to fame. Word of mouth about the quality of the meat pulled in customers from far and wide. The shop was frequently mentioned on Food Network. Still, Jason hadn't expected to find the place open at midnight, especially not on the 4th of July. The lights were on but the door was locked. From the roof, someone yelled, "Around back!"

Jason followed the narrow brick alley to the rear. A police cruiser sat parked next to a dumpster. An iron ladder ran up the two-story building. At the top of the ladder, tiki torches flickered.

"Come on up," someone yelled, though he couldn't see who. He carefully climbed the rusty rungs.

A crowd was jammed onto the roof, filling four large picnic tables. One table held the ghoulish sight of an entire roasted pig, the flesh of its face half picked away to reveal menacing tusks and vacant eye-sockets.

"Oh my God," a fat man in a Hawaiian shirt brayed as he dug into the pig's eye-socket with a fork. "This meat back here—Christ almighty!"

A second fat man at the table knocked back a bottle of Cuervo. Jason recognized him even out of uniform—Doc Law, the local sheriff.

Law wiped his mouth on his forearm and said, loudly, "My friends, in my youth, I traveled Europe. I visited the Sistine Chapel. When I gazed up and beheld that glorious work of Michelangelo, I understood, for the first time in my life, why God had given me eyes. When I journeyed to Vienna and heard Mozart performed in that grand opera house, I understood why God blessed me with ears. And tonight, dear friends, feasting upon this fine swine's cheek, I glimpse God's purpose in giving me a tongue."

Law's speech was met with a simple, "Aw, shucks."

This was spoken by a man in pirate garb, with a capuchin monkey perched on his shoulder. The sight of the pig had been such a draw to Jason's eye that he'd missed both pirate and monkey, partially concealed behind a veil of smoke rising from a large coal-filled drum. Sausages sizzled on a grate above the coals. Next to the drum was a pole that held a realistic human rib cage that bore the hand-painted sign "Dead Man's Chest."

The crowd resumed its conversation as Doc Law went back to devouring pork face. Jason walked to the pirate, who offered a friendly, "Ahoy, matey! Aaahrr!"

"Are you William Kidd?" Jason asked.

"Aye," Kidd answered in pirate drawl, "Who be ye?"

"Jason Rogers." Jason watched Kidd's face to see if there was any reaction to the name. Perhaps his sister had mentioned him. Kidd showed only a pirate grin.

"Want a bratwurst, matey?" Kidd asked. "Or would ye rather grab a fork and pull up to the pig?"

"This is the first time I've seen a roasted pig outside of the movies," Jason said.

Kidd dropped the pirate accent, and said in a more southern drawl, "I use all the pig but the oink. When you kill a creature, there's a duty not to be wasteful."

"I guess," Jason said.

"If there's any left, you should get some of the meat in the eye-socket. Good eats."

"I'll take your word for it," Jason said. "And the sheriff's. He's got quite the silver tongue."

"When he's drinking, the former professor comes out."

"He used to be a professor?"

"Taught literature here at Stanley. Got fired after being accused of trading grades for sex. Instead of leaving town in shame, he used his gift for gab to run for sheriff."

"Huh," said Jason. "I met him last year and took him for a redneck with a word-a-day calendar. Guess I shouldn't judge people by first impressions."

"Why not? Saves time."

"True," said Jason. "Now that I've met you, I don't think this trip has been in vain."

"Oh?"

"I'm dying, Mr. Kidd," Jason said. He dug into his pocket and produced a business card for the butcher shop on which they stood. "You might be my last hope."

He handed Kidd the business card. Kidd looked down, at his own name and title: William Kidd, Meat Artist. Kidd flipped the card over, revealing a handwritten number.

"My cell phone, Mr. Kidd," said Jason. "Why don't you give me a call tomorrow?"

"Um," Kidd said. "If you're dying, what do you want me for? I'm not a doctor. I'm a butcher."

"I know," said Jason.

"I DON'T THINK anything waits after we die," Cassie said.

Cassie was always blurting out stuff like this. They'd just had sex and she was still tied spread-eagle to the bed. Her proper line of dialogue should've been, "That was fantastic!" Kidd would even have been satisfied with, "My arms have fallen asleep."

Kidd had been the one doing all the physical work and was exhausted. He decided not to play into her gratuitous weirdness. He grabbed the butcher knife next to the bed and lunged toward her, slashing the cotton rope that bound her right wrist.

Cassie raised her arm, stretching her fingers.

"That tingles. I love the sensation."

"You can finish the rest." Kidd placed the knife in her free hand and collapsed next to her, halfway to sleep.

"My father has probably putrefied," Cassie said. Her dad had died two months ago. Kidd had never met the man. The main thing he knew was that her father had treated his manic-depressive daughter with prayer instead of Prozac. The result was the strange skinny girl lying next to him. Each time Cassie knocked on his door she sported fresh ink-pen tattoos on paper-white skin. She had skin you could see veins through, stretched over a torso where you could count every rib.

"Rotting seems wasteful," she said, dropping the ropes and knife onto the floor. She curled up next to him, not making any contact. *"Indians left bodies out to be picked over by buzzards."*

"Check Gertrude's food bowl on your way out," Kidd mumbled.

"When I die," Cassie said, *"I'd like to donate my body to a restaurant. Get turned into a stew and have my friends over for a feast."*

Kidd opened his eyes, feeling more alert.

"You don't have any friends," he said.

A POUNDING ON his door woke Kidd mid-afternoon. He rolled out of bed, his head throbbing. Gertrude stretched beside him, dead to the world. She'd gotten into the pina coladas. Pineapple, coconut, rum—a monkey didn't stand a chance.

The pounding continued. Kidd staggered into the living room and yanked the door open.

Doc Law stood outside, fist raised to knock again. Mirrored sunglasses hid his eyes.

"'Sup, Doc," said Kidd, his tongue thick and sticky.

"One of my deputies said he spied Jason Rogers in town. That name mean anything to you?"

Kidd nodded. "He was at the party."

"He was? Why didn't I notice him?"

"You know him?"

Law nodded. "Maybe eight months ago, his sister disappeared. That Goth chick. He came down here and wouldn't leave me alone for a week. He thought she might have been murdered, or worse."

"Hmm," said Kidd. "Well, he's back."

"And at the party?"

"Not more than ten feet from you. Didn't stay long."

"Damn," said Law, shaking his head. "Father Time is taking his toll. In my youth, I could drink gallons of Cuervo and retain my acumen. Ten feet, you say?"

"Yeah. This have anything to do with me?"

"I didn't bother you about this at the time, but Rogers had this baseless theory you were involved with his sister's disappearance. He'd ventured down here to collect her belongings. Took residence at a hotel in Smithfield to search through her stuff. He found one of your business cards."

"Half the people in town have those. More than half."

"I know. There was also some poetry—though given my knowledge of the literary arts I am loathe to use that word. The writings were of a genre moody young women are inexplicably fond of, bad free verse of the 'his love consumes me' type. Morbid-romantic crap, and not a word naming you. It's all about some shadowy, unnamed 'He.' Many would-be poets display a phobia of proper nouns."

Kidd closed his eyes and leaned against the doorframe. Law could meander for hours on poetry. Not believing for a moment it would work, Kidd tried to get Law back on track. "This involves me how?"

"Jason thought that you were 'He,'" Doc Law said. "I gave him my professional opinion. I didn't know Cassie but I'd seen her around. She obviously didn't belong at Stanley. I suspect she took the money from her inheritance and hit the road. Jason wasn't convinced. He found your card among Cassie's effects suspicious because his sister was a vegetarian."

"Big deal," said Kidd. "So am I."

Law's jaw went slack. He rocked back on the heels of his alligator boots, as if he'd been struck. "Surely you jest?"

"Nope. Vegetarian since I was nineteen. Mostly."

"But..."

"Yeah, I know. Butcher, irony, yadda-yadda. Get back to this Roberts guy."

"Rogers. Deputy says he saw him downstairs at noon, trying the door to your shop."

"I'm supposed to be open. I didn't get to bed until 9 this morning."

"There's your mistake," said Law. "I haven't been to bed." Law paused to produce a hip flask, from which he took a swig. He offered the silver flask to Kidd. Fumes wafted from the open mouth.

Kidd's nose wrinkled. "What is that? Paint thinner?"

"Ouzo," said Law. "I'm drinking my way around the world. Momentum serves a man as well as sleep."

"I admire your stamina. I'm going back to bed now."

"Return to your well-deserved slumber. If this fellow becomes a nuisance, you know where to find me."

Kidd nodded, closing the door.

"WE SHOULD TELL *each other our darkest secrets," Cassie said, as Kidd tightened her blindfold.*

"Too easy. You'd confess anything," Kidd said, rubbing her cheek with his gloved hand.

"I lost my virginity when I was thirteen to my best friend Kiera and a cucumber. A week later she died in a wreck. I thought it was God's punishment."

"Okay," Kidd said. Then, deadpan: "That's so shocking. You're such a bad girl."

Cassie pouted. "I'm not trying to shock you. I just want ... I want more intimacy. All we ever do is screw. We never talk."

"You talk all the time," Kidd said.

"I tell you everything," she said, "and you don't give anything back."

Kidd yanked her blindfold off and began untying her.

"What are you doing?" she asked.

"I don't feel like playing," he said. "You're right… I just want the sex. If I want conversation I've got Gertrude."

IT WAS TEN at night when Kidd finally called Jason. Jason said to meet him in front of the butcher shop — he'd have the RV there in two minutes. He asked that Kidd come out to the RV — and, to Kidd's mind, he sounded a little nervous.

"Come on, Gertrude," Kidd said. Gertrude sat on the couch watching *Gilligan's Island*, but looked up alertly as her name was spoken. Kidd nodded and Gertrude sprang from the couch, flying to his shoulder. She landed light as a bag of cement — Gertrude had filled out considerably under his care.

Kidd went down the narrow stairs that led from his apartment into the butcher shop. At the front window headlights were pulling up.

Kidd left the shop, not bothering to lock it, and walked up to the motor home. It was a nice model, very sleek, something you might expect a rich granddad to be driving around Florida.

The door opened.

"Come in," Jason said.

Kidd admired the layout. The RV was all kitchen, a nice one, with a chunky antique butchers block square in the center. This reminded Kidd of his grandfather's butchers block — his father had sold it years ago. His father hadn't had a sentimental bone in him, but Kidd was instantly transported to childhood, watching his grandfather work the meat. He'd never once doubted what he wanted to do with his life.

"Nice table," Kidd said, running his hand along the oiled surface. The wood was scarred with knife marks. It even had cigarette burns along the edge, just like his grandfather's.

"You bring that monkey everywhere?" Jason asked.

"I feel kind of naked without her."

"You let her in the shop?"

"She has a cage. I don't let her roam free. She steals meat and gets aggressive." As Kidd said this, he noted how clean the kitchen was. Jason must be a germ-freak.

"Gertrude is housetrained," he said.

"Oh," said Jason, in a tone that indicated the question hadn't been on his mind.

Jason looked down at the butcher's block, gathering his thoughts. He took a deep breath. "Did I tell you last night that I'm..." His voice trailed off.

"Dying," said Kidd. "What of?"

"Ennui," said Jason. He grinned. "That's my little joke. Brain tumor. I have six months."

"Or longer," Kidd said. "People beat these things."

"I'm not doing chemo," said Jason. "Or any treatment."

"Oh," said Kidd.

"It's counterproductive to pollute my body."

"Counterproductive?"

"Have you thought much about dying, Mr. Kidd?" Jason asked. "More specifically, have you thought about what will happen to your body after death?"

"Not really," said Kidd.

"I have. You might say it's become an obsession of mine. Last year, I visited the Body Works exhibit, in Berlin. You've heard of it?"

Kidd gave a non-committal shrug.

"There's an artist who takes human cadavers and plasticizes them. Turns them into works of art. Not long after my visit, I learned I had a brain tumor. It made think. I'm young. I don't have kids; I have no real legacy to leave the world."

"Did you contact Body Works? See if they can use you?"

"Here's the catch," said Jason. "Due to the nature of my tumor, they won't accept my donation. They're overbooked with donors anyway, but, even if they weren't, the fact I have something wrong with my brain means they can't accept my donation."

"So donate your body to a medical school," said Kidd. "The tumor's a plus."

"I've considered it," said Jason. "It isn't quite the same. It lacks... artistry. The bodies in Berlin—they've transcended the status of corpse. They're art."

"You've given this some thought," said Kidd. "I think I see where you're going with this."

"You're the best butcher in North America," said Jason.

"Aw," said Kidd. "Shucks."

CASSIE RUBBED HER wrists, which felt naked without the ropes. Kidd wouldn't make eye contact.

"You do have a secret, don't you?" she said. "Something awful. You're afraid of it."

Kidd turned away, leaving the bedroom. Cassie paused for a minute, afraid to follow. She dressed slowly before walking into the kitchen. He was standing in front of the coffee maker, nude save for the leather gloves. His nakedness while she was dressed gave her a feeling of power.

"It's only an act," she said. "The dominance. The confidence and control. You aren't even in control of your emotions."

JASON LEFT TOWN empty-handed. Kidd had treated the whole thing as a joke. Still, Jason had seen the gleam in Kidd's eye. Kidd may not have agreed with his words, but his eyes told Jason that Kidd was already planning the menu.

Jason kept a notebook where he recorded all the evidence. It was full of pages of his sister's poetry. It had a Polaroid taken sometime around their father's death. He knew this because Cassie was constantly updating her pen tattoos, and the artwork in the picture was what she'd displayed in the sleeveless black gown she'd worn to the funeral. In the photo, she was blindfolded, tied to a bed, and covered with red bite marks. The photo was frustratingly barren of further clues—the only background was the white sheet.

On the page opposite was a poem entitled "Devoured." It praised her "Master of Meat." Jason wasn't sure how much more the sheriff needed spelled out for him.

The RV was wired with spy cams and tape recorders. He knew in his gut that Kidd had killed his sister. All that was left was to get Kidd to confess. Or, failing that, to get Kidd to agree on tape to kill him. Get irrefutable proof Kidd was capable of the crime.

The rest of July, and through the hot, endless August, Jason haunted a trailer park an hour away from Hog Station, closer to the ocean. He spent his days wandering the small towns near the Carolina coast, quaint tourist destinations like New Bern and Elizabeth City. He sent Kidd postcards, not mentioning what they'd discussed, but making sure Kidd wouldn't forget him.

As September rolled around, he gave Kidd a call.

"Change your mind yet?" he asked.

"I admire your persistence," said Kidd.

"Is that a yes?"

"No. Labor Day's this weekend. I'm up to my neck in special orders. Call me when I'm not so busy."

Jason hung up the phone, satisfied. There was only one reason Kidd would ask that he call back.

KIDD TURNED AROUND, *holding two cups of coffee. He offered Cassie one, she took it.*

"I control the world," Kidd said.

"Tell me one thing," she said. "Tell me something you've never told anyone else."

"I told you I left home when I was 17 and hitchhiked around the world."

"That's not a secret," she said. "That's bragging. But you can't be perfect. There must be something you keep hidden, some dark secret."

"We're in a B&D relationship I won't let you talk about. You're my dark secret."

Cassie sipped her coffee. His dark secret. The words gave her a buzzy, electric feeling in the small of her back. These were the most romantic words she'd ever imagined.

"If that doesn't satisfy you, how's this? When I was nineteen, I ate a man."

Cassie rolled her eyes. He had broken the mood. "A gay encounter? This is your embarrassing secret?"

"No," Kidd said. "I devoured him."

"You devour me," she said, raising her hand to touch her purple hickey.

"I mean I cooked him, chewed him, swallowed him, digested him. He was delicious."

A WEEK BEFORE Halloween, Kidd met Jason on Highway 70, thirty miles from Hog Station, where people were less likely to recognize him. It was a chill day. The sky hung gray and low.

They drove out to Atlantic Beach. They didn't talk much. When Jason tried to go over the plan one last time, Kidd said, "I know the plan," ending the conversation. Even Gertrude was quiet.

Jason was frustrated. Kidd always did this—he would never say the words Jason needed him to say: *"The plan is, we fake your suicide, I bring you back to the RV and kill you with your homemade electric chair, then I butcher you and sell the meat in my shop."*

Of course, the homemade electric chair was a fake. Once he had Kidd on camera pulling the switch, he would pull out the gun hidden under the seat and make a citizen's arrest. He was tempted to cut to the chase and use the gun to force Kidd to confess to Cassie's murder, or even at least to knowing her, but he suspected that might not stand up in court.

Night had fallen by the time they reached Fort Macon, at the tip of the island. The parking lot was empty. Together they drug out the inflatable boat. They waited in the mist as the electric pump filled the rubberized canvas with air.

Gertrude pressed against the windshield, watching them work. When the boat was fully inflated, they carried it down to the sand.

It was high tide. Waves churned in the inlet, as the water of the sound rushed into the Atlantic. A boat launched now would be carried out to sea.

Jason dropped his suicide note into the boat.

"It says I only have weeks left, that I don't want to still be alive when my mind goes."

Jason bent over the boat and produced a box cutter. Silently, teeth clenched, he ran the blade across his open palm. A line of blood bubbled up. He touched the canvas, leaving a bloody handprint. He shook his hand, sending blood drops all around the boat.

"No one will ever know the truth," he said.

Jason waded into the waves. He stood there, in water up to his waist, as the current carried the boat away.

Jason turned and waded back to the beach. He said, "So far, things have gone pretty well."

Kidd didn't answer. It was dark save for the headlights. As Jason trod back onto the shore, Kidd was little more than a silhouette.

Jason walked to him, looking at his hand. "This really stings."

He looked up. Kidd loomed over him, his left arm raised. He held a cleaver from his shop, big and heavy, its sharp edge gleaming. With a grunt that made Jason cringe, Kidd swung.

"HIS NAME WAS Big Mike. He was an Eastern Islander, making a living as a bush pilot in Alaska. I bummed a ride with him, trying to get to Kaktovic, a little village as far North as you can get. I got a little nervous when Mike lit up a joint ten minutes into the flight, but figured he was a pro. Except he wasn't. He crashed the plane into a valley. We were lucky to survive. The first couple of days, we kept thinking rescue might arrive any minute. After a week, we knew no one was looking for us. He'd been kind of lax

filing flight plans. We made a little shelter out of the plane fuselage — and there were trees around, so we had a fire, and melted snow for water. But, we were hungry. Big Mike kept making these crazy jokes. He weighed, like, 300 pounds, I weighed maybe 130. I was going to go before he did. He said that when I went, he'd eat me. Said among his people, they called the white man 'long pig.'

"So I killed him. Then I ate him. I confessed to the park ranger *who found me a month later. He said he saw no reason either of us should ever mention it.*"

Cassie shook her head. "If you can't be serious, I'm wasting my time."

Kidd shrugged. "If talking doesn't work for you, we could always go back to bed and tie you up."

Cassie sighed. "Okay."

IT WAS HALLOWEEN morning when Kidd got the mail. It was postmarked from a week before. Inside was a letter and a videotape.

"Kidd," the letter began:

"If you are reading this, something went wrong with my plan. Perhaps I'm dead. You haven't won. I know what you did to my sister. You'll rot in Hell for what you've done.

"More immediately, you'll rot in prison. I never had a brain tumor. I've been playing you like a violin, Mr. Kidd. I've videotaped every visit. I've recorded every phone call. You've been slick and evasive, but I still have an impressive body of evidence. All that evidence is now in the hands of the sheriff and the FBI, who've received identical packages. With luck, I'm still alive, and have delivered even more evidence to them. If I've not been lucky, and somehow you've killed me, I take comfort in knowing that my sacrifice will lead to bringing you to justice.

"Checkmate, Mr. Kidd."

Kidd sat the letter down on the table, went back into the kitchen, and resumed work on the slab of meat resting on the antique butchers block. He had a ton of work to do in preparation for tonight's festivities. Kidd chuckled as the full impact of Jason's scheme sunk in. What a melodramatic little prick.

"You're pretty skinny," Kidd said, studying Cassie's naked body. "Some decent meat on your legs, but, really, you're mostly bone. I guess I could fry up the skin. Make cracklin's. Use the rest of you for sausage and stew."

"You wouldn't use me for barbecue?" she asked, pouting.

He stroked the skin below her tiny breasts, feeling the ribs. "Not enough fat," he said. "You'd be too dry."

"I feel so wet," she said, arching her back as he knelt over her. "Promise me you'll eat me when I die."

"I'm going to eat you right now," he said, rubbing the edge of the knife along her cheek without cutting her.

Her breath caught in her throat, and she shuddered with pleasure.

Doc Law eased his cruiser down Main Street, enjoying the spectacle. Stanley College frowned upon Halloween festivities. This led the students to put extra care and effort into their masks. For one night a year, Hog Station reminded Law of Brazil's Carnival.

Law pulled his cruiser next to the dumpster behind Kidd's Meats. A half-dozen girls gathered here, smoking Lucky Strikes at the base of the ladder. They sported elaborate masks decorated with fur and feathers, and nothing else save body paint. Earlier in the night, he could tell, the women had been jungle cats—the orange and tan paints that covered them had been decorated with broad black stripes and spots. Now, the paint that covered their breasts and buttocks was smudged into a muddy gray. Law tipped his hat to them as he passed.

"Ladies," he said.

On the rooftop, Doc Law found a jungle. The tiki torches along the roof's edge lit dozens of potted banana plants, their broad green leaves casting strange shadows.

At the rear of the roof sat a bamboo shack. A crude sign on a board read, "Cannibal Kidd's Manburgers." Kidd stood next to an enormous iron pot, big enough to hold at least two missionaries, perhaps three. The stew within bubbled over a propane burner, giving the night a meaty, peppery odor. Kidd wore a palm frond skirt and a bone through his nose. Gertrude hung from the roof of the shack, greedily eyeing the stew.

"This might be the least politically correct display I've ever seen," Law said, approaching Kidd.

"I'd offer you a manburger," said Kidd, "but the tigresses cleaned me out. Business has been brisk. I'm down to stew, mostly."

"That's fine," said Law. "Smells good."

"I know," said Kidd. "Still, I might have something better suited to a man of your refined tastes."

"Do tell."

"Last July, when you were eating the pig's head—did you get any of the eye? Or did the mayor finish it off?"

"The mayor devoured it quicker than I could react," said Law. "He has the table manners of a wood chipper."

"Step back here," said Kidd.

Law followed Kidd behind the bamboo shack. On the edge of the roof was a small brazier, the charcoal within glowing red. Kidd knelt to a styrofoam cooler and opened the lid. Resting on the ice were two eyeballs, the meat still attached.

Law felt a little queasy as Kidd stuck a bamboo skewer through each eye, then placed them over the coals. The eyes sizzled as they touched the hot iron, and the smell that filled the air instantly banished all queasiness. Law searched for words to describe the smell, but words failed. It wasn't beef, exactly, nor the smell of pork. It was something different, more substantial. His mouth watered.

After a minute, Kidd sprinkled a pinch of salt and pepper as he flipped the skewers by hand. The eyeballs deflated, the jelly within dripping onto the charcoal, giving the smoke a richness and complexity that again robbed Law of vocabulary.

"You shouldn't over spice these," Kidd said, wiping his hands on his grass skirt. "The meat speaks for itself."

"Sweet Jesus," Law said. "If I don't put that in my mouth soon I might go mad."

"Patience," Kidd said.

After a long minute, Kidd lifted a skewer, testing the meat with his finger. He smiled. "They're done."

Kidd offered Law a skewer. Law took the meat and raised it to his trembling lips.

The taste was explosive—salty, smoky, greasy. The flesh of the eyeball was charred and crisp, crackling between his teeth. The meat around the eye—it defined meat. This *was* meat. All that he'd ever eaten before paled.

The meat melted on his tongue. Law closed his eyes and groaned, savoring the moment, swaying. He felt himself dissolving. He could no longer remember his name. He grew aware of his transcendent connection to everything. He was the spoke of a grand, ceaseless wheel, where the sun rose and fell, rose and fell, warming the carnivores of the world as they devoured their trembling prey. He was the center, holding. The moment stretched on, his body vibrating, until he heard a crunch.

He opened his eyes to find Kidd chewing the other eyeball.

As Kidd swallowed, Law watched his throat with a hungry gaze. Kidd's eyes were closed and Law studied his face. It seemed radiant, beatific—even holy. Law focused on Kidd's mouth—his youthful lips full and pink, gleaming with the grease of the now vanished meat. A few flecks of black pepper rested on the lips, and a single, shining crystal of salt sat at the crease of the mouth, tempting, enticing. Law wanted to lean forward, to place his lips on Kidd's lips, to run his tongue along the grease, the pepper, the salt, to suck out the echo of the eye that lingered in Kidd's saliva. Alas, there are social norms that render certain actions taboo, and these taboos are mighty, mightier even than eyeball consumption euphoria.

Law broke the uncomfortable intimacy by mumbling, "So much for you being a vegetarian."

Kidd slowly opened his eyes, returning from whatever heaven the meat had transported him to. He stared blankly at Law as he processed the words. He smirked.

"I said mostly."

"Hey Kidd," a voice called from the other side of the shack. "Is the stew self serve or what? I see your damn monkey's been sampling it."

It was the mayor—his brash voice was instantly recognizable.

"Help yourself, Mayor," Kidd said.

Kidd looked at Law. "You want some stew?"

"After what I've just had, I fear it would only disappoint."

Kidd looked hurt.

"I mean no offense," said Law. "You are a cook of incomparable artistry, and I have no doubt that the stew is pure ambrosia. It's just..."

"No need to explain," said Kidd. "I felt the same the first time I tasted it."

Law nodded. A long second of silence passed between them, then another. There was something that needed to be said, but neither of them wanted to go first.

In the end, it was Kidd who risked the question.

"So, did you get...?"

"Yes," said Law. "This morning."

"Watch the video?"

"Yes. He put some work into this."

"And?" Kidd asked.

"They found a boat washed up on Shackleford Banks," said Law. "It held a suicide note. If the blood tests as his, the case is closed in my book. And the FBI isn't going to waste time on some nut-job's delusions."

"He was crazy, you know," said Kidd.

"I can't say that I know that," said Law. "But I do know one thing. I've tasted what you can do with meat."

Kidd shrugged, looking modest.

Law licked his lips, tasting the memory. "No fair man could judge it a crime."

SECRET ORIGINS

A friend of mine named Cathy Bollinger challenged me to write a story about a small town cannibal. I decided that the only way I could approach it was to try to make the reader hungry. Which meant I had to spend a lot of time daydreaming about what people would taste like using various cooking techniques. And getting really hungry.

I think there's something wrong with me.

WHERE THEIR WORM DIETH NOT

ATOMAHAWK TOOK A PACK of unfiltered Camels from his utility belt and popped a fresh cigarette between his lips. His fingertip glowed like a miniature sun as he lit it. Acrid smoke curled toward Retaliator.

Retaliator, squatting on the edge of the roof of the vacant factory, said nothing as he stared down at the docks of the darkened warehouse. It was two in the morning; it had been at least twenty minutes since the last goon had furtively slipped inside. Despite Retaliator's focused silence, something in his posture must have changed imperceptibly.

"What?" said Atomahawk, sounding defensive.

"What what?" Retaliator answered, keeping his voice gravelly and neutral, still not looking at his long-time ally.

"You flinched when I lit up," said Atomahawk. "You've got a problem with my smoking?"

"I'm not here pass judgment," said Retaliator, who recognized the irony of the statement. The whole reason he was a crime-fighter was that he was willing to judge people. This was why he spent nights skulking dark alleys in dangerous parts of town rather than drinking brandy by the fireplace in his mansion. He was well-known for his ability to see things clearly, in black in white, cutting through the haze of gray fog that afflicted so many of his fellow men. He sighed.

"A: Lighting your cigarette with your powers is about as stealthy as waving around a road flare. B: Kids look up to the Law Legion and you're the most powerful member. If they see you smoking, they'll think it's okay. C: You're my friend, John. You deserve a better death than lung cancer."

Atomahawk nodded as he hovered closer to the roof's edge. John Naiche was a full-blooded Apache who looked quite striking in his bright-red plastisteel armor. His long black hair flowed like a cape down his back. He'd been a founding member of the Law Legion along with Retaliator, Arc, She-Devil and Tempo. The big Apache took a long draw on the cigarette, then flicked it away.

He crossed his arms and said, "You know I took it up again right after your last funeral."

"Again?" asked Retaliator.

Atomahawk furrowed his brow, puzzled by the query. Unlike Retaliator, he wore no mask to hide his features, only war paint that looked like swept-back hawk's wings.

"You said 'again,'" said Retaliator. "It implies you used to smoke before."

"Oh," said Atomahawk. "Yeah. In high-school. I quit when I joined the marines. But for the last ten years, any time I get stressed out, I can't help but think about putting a cigarette in my mouth. The last time Prime Mover killed you, I bummed one from a teenager outside the funeral home. I haven't been able to stop. Honestly, why should I worry? My blood is more radioactive than uranium. I have to bury my feces in lead jars because they'd kill any ordinary man that got near them. Cancer's coming, but it's the radiation that will do me in, not cigarettes."

Retaliator struggled not to roll his eyes. He'd heard Atomahawk's *my-power-is-my-curse shtick* often enough he could recite it by rote.

A long moment of silence passed as they both stared at the warehouse.

Atomahawk said, "Anyway, I'm not the most powerful Legionnaire anymore. She-Devil's scary now that she's eaten Satan's heart. And Golden Victory could probably take me in a fight, if it came to it."

"I could take you in a fight," said Retaliator. "It doesn't change the fact that kids look up to you."

"You dress like a refugee from a bondage flick," said Atomahawk. "Don't lecture me about corrupting children. How's Nubile doing, by the way?"

Retaliator pressed his lips together tightly. "She's off the respirator," he said softly, losing the deep raspy baritone he normally affected. "The doctor's say... they say she might recover more brain function in time. It's still too early to know."

"That's good," said Atomahawk, in a tone that meant, "That sucks."

Retaliator stood up, stretching his back. He tugged up his leather pants, which had slipped down a bit. Perhaps he did look a bit like a bondage fanatic in his black leather pants, knee high boots with about a hundred silver buckles, leather gloves that laced up his forearms, and a black mask that concealed all his features save for zippered slits at the eyes, mouth, and nostrils. His shaved chest was completely bare, showing off the hundreds of scars he'd acquired over twenty-years of crime-fighting. His skin wasn't bullet-proof, but his entire cardio-vascular system was composed of high-tech bio-plastics from the 28th century that few 21st century weapons could damage.

His outfit, he knew, made some people uncomfortable. But they'd been the clothes his father, Reinhart Gray, former chief justice of the Supreme Court, had been found dead in. Police had ruled his death accidental, saying he was the victim of auto-erotic asphyxiation. Eric Gray had become the Retaliator in order to solve the mystery of his father's murder, a quest for justice that still drove him twenty-years later. Wearing his father's clothes wasn't a sexual statement. It was, instead, a warning to the unknown murderer, a reminder that there was one man, at least, who still remembered his crime.

"Here comes Casper," said Atomahawk.

"Don't call him that," growled Retaliator.

The ethereal form of Witness floated toward the roof. Witness was really Chang Williams, the ghost of a twelve-year-old conjoined twin whose now-separated brother was currently trapped in a coma. Chang's spirit was trapped on earth, unseen by all save for the few souls who'd been to the other side and returned. Since nearly all the members of the Law Legion had died at one point or another, they'd recently adopted the ghost-child and given him a new life as Witness, an invisible, intangible spy who could gather information in the most dangerous environments without risk to himself.

Witness floated before them, completely naked, since souls have no need for clothes. It was politically incorrect to call conjoined twins Siamese, yet, Chang was, in fact, from Thailand, formerly known as Siam, though he'd been raised in America. He was thin, almost girlish, having died before puberty, with skin the color of a walnut shell; his dark eyes had no irises as he stared at Retaliator and said, "There are a dozen men inside. They frighten me. I can't touch them."

"You can't touch anybody," said Atomahawk.

Witness reached out and placed his skinny fingers onto the Apache's boot. The big man gave a small yelp and jerked his foot away. "What the hell was that?"

"You should read the dossiers. Witness has a graveyard touch," growled Retaliator. "He can brush against anyone's soul and make them feel the mortal chill of their own guilt."

"So, what, the men in that warehouse have no souls?" asked Atomahawk.

"They've signed Prime Mover's contract," said Retaliator, with a sigh. "Another dozen lost to the God Clock."

"They're well armed," said Witness. "Assault rifles and fancy-looking pistols. They've got cases of C4 in the back of the warehouse. Also, five or six small helicopters. At least I think they're helicopters; they don't have rotors attached. They're planning to blow something up, but no one said what."

"The Supreme Court," said Retaliator.

"Is this anything more than a guess?" said Atomahawk.

"Tomorrow is when they're hearing arguments on Prime Mover's appeals. They're being asked to decide if a murder conviction can stand if the victim is later restored to life by a time-travel paradox."

"Even if he gets off on that technicality, he's guilty of hundreds of other murders," said Atomahawk. "He's not going to walk. And why blow up a hearing that might lead to a ruling in his favor?"

"It's too big of a coincidence that his goons are stocking up on explosives. Security is going to be high tomorrow. He would blow the place up just to prove he still runs the world, even from a prison cell."

"Is he that crazy?"

"Maybe," said Retaliator. "Or maybe the guy rotting in prison isn't the real Prime Mover. When they put him in jail, Prime Mover claimed he was a cop named Jason Reid who'd somehow been put into Prime Mover's body. An hour later, though, he was back to normal. Assuming normal is the right word for a man who believes he's God."

"You're taking the idea he can swap his soul into other bodies seriously?" asked Atomahawk.

"I'm talking to the ghost of a Siamese twin and an Indian with a fusion reactor where his heart should be," said Retaliator. "I'm not in a position to dismiss anything as impossible."

Atomahawk nodded toward the warehouse. "We going to do this thing?"

"Go," said Retaliator. "Make it loud."

Retaliator jumped onto his zip line and slid down to the dumpsters behind the warehouse as Atomahawk blazed through the night sky like a comet. He landed on the dumpster as a thunderous crack came from the front of the warehouse. The ground shook as the steel door near the dumpster blew from its hinges, a victim of the rapid change in air pressure inside the building as Atomahawk blasted through the front doors.

Retaliator's muscles tensed. He toyed with the closed switchblade in his palm. Any second, at least one of the goons would make the sensible decision to flee. That would be Retaliator's cue to drag him into the dumpster and have a few private moments during which he would make the goon tell everything he knew about Prime Mover's plans.

The seconds passed in odd silence. Normally by now hired muscle would be shooting at Atomahawk, not believing in his well-documented invulnerability. Nothing short of an anti-space grenade was going to hurt Atomahawk, and Retaliator was certain that he was in possession of the last of the five prototype grenades built before Professor Novy had died.

A full minute went by. Someone stuck his head out of the door. It was Atomahawk.

"You should take a look at this," he said.

Retaliator jumped from the dumpster and looked into the warehouse.

The vast space was well lit by a few atomaflares drifting in the air. The warehouse was completely empty. There weren't even any cobwebs.

"I've scanned all spectrums. Nothing is hiding invisibly. There's chaotic heat residue from people who were here, but I'm afraid I wiped out any useful IR information with the blast that took out the front doors."

"I swear they were here two minutes ago," said Witness, who'd joined them.

Retaliator sighed as he rubbed the bridge of his nose through his mask. "Prime Mover must have activated another power of the God Clock. Teleportation? Time Travel?"

"She-Devil might know the next power," said Atomahawk. "She was around when they built the Antikythera mechanism."

"Go to DC," said Retaliator. "Keep an eye on the courthouse."

"They aren't going to let me anywhere near the building," said Atomahawk.

"That's why you have a secret identity," said Retaliator.

"I'm six-foot five, I don't wear a mask, and I set off Geiger counters from twenty feet away," said Atomahawk. "My secret identity isn't as useful as yours, rich boy."

"Figure out something," said Retaliator.

Witness said, "It's no problem for me to get in. I'll contact you the second I spot anything suspicious." He faded from sight, back into the ghoststream.

Atomahawk lifted into the air. "It might not be him," he said.

"It's always him," said Retaliator. "Every time I think Prime Mover is finished, he comes back stronger than ever."

"Lucky thing for the world you're always waiting for him," said Atomahawk.

"Yeah," said Retaliator, his shoulders sagging, as leaned against the dumpster.

"What?" asked Atomahawk, pausing twenty feet up.

"What what?" asked Retaliator.

"You look so down. This isn't like you."

Retaliator reached back and unzipped his mask. He tugged it off, letting the chill November night cool his sweaty hair. "How do you know it's not like me? What makes you think you know anything about me?"

"I've watched you die three times and seen you get married twice," said Atomahawk with a wry smile. "I've literally been to hell and back with you, man. If I don't know you, who does?"

Retaliator scratched the callus on his neck left by the mask.

"So what was it about my last funeral?"

"That made me start smoking again?" said Atomahawk.

"Yeah."

He shrugged. "The first time we thought you were dead, it was right after the Snarthling invasion. Half of the Law Legion still had alien duplicates running around, so, it wasn't a big surprise when we pulled the real you out of the goo-coffin on that captured saucer. The second time, of course, we both died when Dr. Novy blasted us with the anti-space grenades, and we were too busy fighting our way our of hell for me to get stressed out. But the third time you died ... I thought it had really happened. We didn't know you'd been pulled into the twenty-eighth century by Fan Boy, and that the corpse we buried was only a matter-balancing time-echo. It felt final. I should have known it wasn't. We Law Legionnaires never stay dead."

"Or the villians," said Retaliator, shaking his head wearily. "I've seen Prime Mover get torn apart by alligators. I've watched him fall from planes, get run over by a tank, get shot by his own henchman, and decapitated by a helicopter. I get a few months of something almost like peace ... then he's back again. It never ends."

"People come back," said Atomahawk. "It's a crazy world."

"My father didn't come back," said Retaliator. "Amelia didn't come back."

Atomahawk's face fell. He said, apologetically, "I didn't mention the weddings to—"

"Torture me?" said Retaliator. Not a day went by when thoughts of his shattered lovers didn't haunt him. His first wife, Amelia, had taken too many sleeping pills; she'd found out the truth of his second life and never learned to cope with the stress of knowing where her husband really spent his nights. His second wife had known the truth, of course. When Nubile had joined the Law Legion she told everyone she was nineteen, although, in truth, she was fourteen, exactly half Retaliator's age at the time. She'd passed as older due to her shape-shifting. Fortunately, the first four years they'd fought side-by-side, their relationship had never advanced past teasing flirtation. When they'd finally taken off their masks and progressed to the next phase, Retaliator was no longer technically a pedophile.

"I'm not trying to torture anyone," said Atomahawk. "Don't let events bring you down, is all I'm saying. We're fighting the good fight. A war can't be judged by a single battle."

"Get to DC," said Retaliator, pulling his mask back on. "We've got work to do. I'm going to talk to She-Devil."

AS ATOMAHAWK VANISHED into the night sky, Retaliator walked to the nearest manhole cover. "Going to talk to She-Devil" was both the easiest and the hardest thing in the world. She-Devil claimed to be Uruk, a five-thousand-year-old woman who'd met Satan in Mesopotamia and broken his heart after a torrid love affair. As a result, he'd cursed her with eternal life and his own duty of punishing the souls of the wicked. But, save for her inability to die, he hadn't given her any special powers to carry out her mission. Thus, she'd started her career constantly drawn to confront the wickedest men on earth without any true power to harm them. Her first thousand years had been hellish, as she'd fallen again and again into the hands of men so vile and depraved they made Ghengis Khan look well-adjusted. Unfortunately for Satan, he'd underestimated the human ability to adapt. Angels and demons were created knowing everything they would ever know. They had little capacity to learn. Humans, on the other hand, improved with age. As the centuries went by, Uruk became nearly unbeatable in hand to hand combat, and eventually mastered the mystic arts as well.

Arc and Tempo had a conspiracy theory that She-Devil had formed the Law Legion specifically so that they could all be killed by Dr. Novy and sent to hell to serve as allies in her final battle with Satan. It was too much for Retaliator to think about, to be honest. Before the Law Legion, his career had consisted of beating up muggers and drug-dealers. It was easy to make the judgment that a man peddling junk to school kids deserved to have his teeth pounded from his mouth. Moral clarity became more difficult when he was called upon to judge alien bureaucrats, time-traveling machine men, and anti-matter refugees from the seventh dimension.

Retaliator rolled aside the manhole cover and beamed his flashlight down into the darkness. Below him was nothing but the muck of a storm drain. He leapt, pulling his arms in as he dropped through the hole. He landed, not in knee-deep water, but in a large cavern lit by the reddish glow of the lava river that bisected it. This was the Devil Cave, filled with memorabilia gathered over five millennia of adventures. The place looked like a graveyard for props from a thousand B-movies. He jumped across the lava river and approached the golden throne. Supposedly, Midas himself had used this chair.

"I know you're here," said Retaliator. "I couldn't be here if you weren't."

"I was just waiting for you to say 'hello,'" a woman's voice answered behind him.

"Hello," he said, turning around.

Retaliator was a tall man at 6'3", but She-Devil was at least a head taller, and taller still if you counted the long black horns curving up from her brow. Her skin was red; not American flag-stripe red like Atomahawk's armor, but blood-red. A pair of leathery wings jutted from her shoulders. She wore armor made from black scales of the dragon she'd slain when they'd escaped hell together.

"What bring you here, Eric?" Her voice was disturbingly normal coming from a black-lipped mouth with white fangs flashing within. She sounded like a gray-haired librarian from Kansas, not an immortal vanquisher of evil. She was also the only one of the Law Legion to ever call him by his first name.

"I need you to tell me what you know about the Antikythera Mechanism."

"Which one?" she asked.

"There's more than one?"

"Of course. There's the original that was pulled out of its watery grave as little more than a slab, and the new one built by the Red Alchemist from the gamma-ray analysis of the old one, then stolen by Prime Mover."

"That's the one. The God Clock. The last time Prime Mover had it in his possession, he fed it one-hundred souls to move the Heaven Wheel and it gave him the power of invisibility. What's the next power on the wheel?"

"What does it matter?" asked She-Devil. "The God-Clock is safely locked away in the pit of souls."

"Is it?"

She frowned. "I know that Prime Mover keeps getting trickier, but, really, he's only a delusional old man once you strip away his gizmos. There's no way he could have stolen the mechanism."

"What's the next power?"

"Soul walking, but—"

"Soul walking?"

"It would allow him to exchange his mind and soul with that of another person for a one hour period."

"So the man in prison—"

"No," said She-Devil. "It's him. A body swap could only last an hour. Even if he had the power, he's been in prison for months."

"Would his victims recall what had happened during that hour?"

She shrugged. "These things don't really come with instruction manuals."

"What's next on the wheel? After soul-walking?"

"Extra-dimensional portals. You could use the wheel to create an unseen gate into a hidden dimension. Sort of like my Devil Cave, or the pit of souls, which is a hidden dimension inside a hidden dimension."

"Show me the mechanism," he said.

She rolled her eyes, in a fashion that reminded him of Amelia when she was exasperated. "Fine," she said, taking a seat on the throne. She used her long black fingernail to trace a circle in the air. Then, she poked the circle in the center, as if the air was a sheet of glass that she'd just cut a hole into. The air fell away in a jumble of sharp-edged fragments leaving a perfect black circle behind.

A chill wind cut through the Devil Cave, moaning like lost souls. She reached her hand into the hole. Her lips pressed together as her eyes narrowed.

"It's gone, isn't it?" said Retaliator.

She gave him a look that chilled his soul. In the many years he'd fought by her side, never once had he seen her eyes filled with fear.

"He possessed you," said Retaliator. "He'd already activated the soul-walking before we captured him. He possessed you and retrieved the God Clock. When the hour was up, you didn't remember."

"That's not—"

"Don't you dare say that's not possible!" snapped Retaliator. "It's the only thing that makes sense!"

Her red cheeks turned pink as the blood drained from her face. She closed the portal as she slumped into her chair.

"There … there was a day, back in August, when I woke up in my mortal form of Eula Leahy and I had no memory of what I'd done the night before."

"You didn't find this unusual? You didn't think this might be worth mentioning to your teammates? You're the most powerful woman in the world. You skewered Satan with his own sword! Don't you think it might be important to keep track of where you are and what you're doing at all times?"

"Don't judge me, Eric," she said, her voice little more than a whisper. "You haven't lived my life. You've never seen the horrors I've seen. Sometimes… sometimes in order to get to sleep, I have a drink or two or three. It's something… it's something I'm in control of… most of the time."

Retaliator took a long, slow breath. Sometimes, it was difficult to remember that underneath all the magic, She-Devil was only a woman doing a job she didn't want to do.

"Look," he said. "The next time you feel like your only hope of getting some peace is a bottle, give me a call. We're teammates, Eula. I'll drop whatever I'm doing and talk you through the darkness."

She responded with a dry chuckle. "For the sake of the world, let's hope that my mood is never so dark that I need to turn to the Retaliator for a pep talk. Leave here, Eric. I need to do further research. There will be forces at play in this cave which no mere mortal can witness and hope to retain his sanity."

"Fine," said Retaliator, "but —"

But he was talking to a wall. He was back in Gray Manor in his own bedroom, facing the Annie Leibowitz portrait of himself and Nubile on their wedding day. It's funny; he knew Sarah first as Nubile, and even now thought of her by that name, even though she would never fight crime again after Prime Mover had put three bullets into the base of her skull. Without her powers, she'd likely be dead. As it was, she was merely an empty shell who didn't understand what people were saying to her in the few moments a day she drifted into wakefulness. She would never be Nubile again. She might never be Sarah again.

He sat on the edge of the bed and pulled off his mask as tears rolled down his cheeks. He lived in a world where a select subgroup of people never really died. He'd cheated death three times, Atomahawk had been dead twice, and Reset's whole power was resurrecting himself; he sometimes died two or three times a day.

He knew, he knew, he knew that these were the exceptions, that every single day thousands of ordinary people died, and stayed dead. It made his pain so much sharper to know that he was alive while his father was still dead from strangulation, and he was alive while his mother was still dead from cancer, and he was alive after Amy has swallowed all those pills and choked on her own vomit. And Sarah, poor Sarah—why was she a vegetable while he was walking around healthier than ever thanks to a heart from the future?

He wiped his cheeks and sucked up the pain, turning the leather mask in his hands, until his true face stared up at him, judging, the empty eye slots full of scorn.

He rose, pulled on a robe that hung down to his ankles, and walked down the hall. He squinted as he stepped through the door at the end, moving from lamp light into overly-bright florescent whiteness. The last three rooms of the wing had been transformed into a private hospital. On the other side of the glass, a doctor looked up at him, then turned away.

He went to her room.

Sarah Kontis Gray was sleeping in her white hospital bed. The room was oddly silent now that the respirator had been removed. The nurse by the bedside, a thin black woman with streaks of gray in her hair, rose as he entered.

"She's been sleeping well," she whispered.

He nodded. In truth, though, he didn't believe the words. In the three years they'd been together, he'd never seen Nubile sleep on her back. She always slept on her side, with her head pressed up against his shoulder. She looked so wrong on her back, with every muscle slack. The crisp white linens lay neatly across her. Normally when she slept, she was murder on blankets, tugging and tucking and stuffing them under body parts until everything was just right.

"Thank you," Eric whispered, as he turned away.

If he wanted to find comfort for his aching soul, this was not the place to look for it. He walked to the library, activated the hidden elevator, and rode down to the quiet room. He tossed the robe aside and pulled on his mask. The door slid open on the stone-lined chamber.

Lawrence David Rambo was slumped on the stone floor, snoring. His ankle was red and raw where the iron manacle held it. He was naked save for the leather bands around his neck and wrists. His body was covered with welts and purple bruises haloed in yellow.

Lawrence David Rambo wasn't a super-villain. He was a petty scoundrel, seventeen-years old, from a suburb near Baltimore. He'd discovered it was easy money to wave a gun around in small mom-and-pop stores out in the boonies, where he'd get away with a hundred bucks if he was lucky, a case of beer, maybe a roll of scratch-off lottery tickets. He'd never shot anyone, but he'd pistol whipped a sixty-year-old woman who hadn't been moving fast enough, and had once pointed his gun at an eight-year-old boy who'd been coming out of the restroom, forcing him to lie down and count to a hundred, shouting that if he stopped counting he'd die.

Lawrence David Rambo was white. His parents were middle-class. He'd been arrested twice for trivial crimes, but never even spent a full night in jail. He was the sort of kid the broken justice system would allow to slip through the cracks until he killed someone.

Retaliator doused him with a bucket of cold water.

The young man gasped awake, trembling.

"Ohgoddon't," he whimpered as he curled into a fetal position. "Ohpleaseohpleasedon't."

Retaliator looked down through his zippered eye-slits at the very worst of humanity. When other men thought of evil, they thought of villains like Hitler, or Osama bin Laden, or Prime Mover. But Retaliator saw the truth. The true evil of the world was insidious in its smallness, the petty, pointless meanness that would pistol whip a grandmother or badger a crying child. The big evils of the world were easy to manage. Armies were sent after men like bin Laden. But the same governments that raised the armies would provide lawyers to men like Rambo, sub-human scum who had hurt people not for any grand plan of world conquest, but simply because it was easy to bully those weaker than him.

Save for his rebuilt heart, Retaliator possessed no superpowers. What allowed him to stand beside demigods like Atomahawk was clarity of vision. He could see through the veil of excuses and justifications that society wove to hide the reality of the evil in their midst.

Eric Gray's great power was his ability to see the world in black and white.

He selected a bullwhip from the wall, its tip studded with shards of broken glass. His prisoner released a series of incoherent whimpers that Retaliator recognized as pleas for mercy.

Retaliator dropped his voice to a cold bass rumble. "Begging will only make me beat you harder."

The young man slowly stilled his voice in a series of choked sobs.

"Or perhaps it's silence that will infuriate me," said Retaliator, raising the whip, knowing, in truth, nothing the boy did mattered any more. He would never leave this room alive.

AS ERIC GRAY, it was simple enough to obtain a seat in the gallery of the Supreme Court, even at the last second. She-Devil was in her human identity of Eula Leahy and accompanied him as his guest. Ordinarily if he was seen around town in the company of a woman, it would be fodder for the tabloids, but Eula really was a small town librarian from Kansas who looked to be in her mid-sixties. In her gray pantsuit, she was nearly invisible in her normalness.

"Where's Atomahawk?" she whispered as they took their seats.

"Fifty miles straight up," Eric whispered back. "He can be here inside of five seconds once Prime Mover's thugs show."

"If they come," said Eula. "Prime Mover stands a good chance of prevailing. Why would he pull something big like this?"

Retaliator didn't answer her question before the bailiff called the room to silence and ordered everyone to rise. The nine judges filed into the room. Eric felt a stirring of sadness as he watched their black robes sway. He remembered his father's robes from long ago.

Eight of the judges sat.

The chief justice, Lucas Shoen, remained standing. With a swift motion, a silver revolver dropped into his hand from his black sleeve. He placed the gun against his temple.

"Bring me the Law Legion," he said, in a crisp British accent that Eric recognized immediately. There was a flurry of confusion as the guards stationed around the rooms drew their guns. Eric grabbed Eula and pushed her to the floor, hiding behind the benches.

"How could he soul-swap with Schoen?" Eula whispered. "When would they ever make eye contact? Prime Mover's still in jail! I checked the magic mirror before I came here."

Eric instantly saw the only possible answer. "The power must work no matter what body he's in. He could jump from person to person for months, swapping every hour, until he arrived in the body he wanted... to ..." His voice trailed off. "You have to leave," he said.

Eula nodded, understanding. There was circumstantial evidence he'd possessed her once. She was among the most difficult of the Law Legion to track down; this whole event could have been staged just for the chance to possess her again.

In the time it took Eric to blink, Eula had vanished, slipping back into the Devil Cave.

Eric reached under the bench and grabbed his utility belt. There had been no way to get through security while wearing it... which is why he'd had Tempo time-walk into the building at five in the morning to plant it. He jammed micro-filters into his nostrils, then crushed a sleeping gas pellet between his fingers. The people immediately around him fell like flies. Seconds later, people cried out in panic as the gas spread, incapacitating everyone. Retaliator pulled on his mask and sprinkled his 5000 dollar suit with the nanites he'd taken from Mothmaster. Instantly the wool fell to dust, revealing his costume. He fastened his utility belt as he stood, palming a concussion grenade.

Nearly everyone in the room had fallen now, save for the chief justice, who was held conscious by the full power of Prime Mover's nearly matchless will.

"Hello, Eric," said Prime Mover.

Retaliator didn't blink.

"Surprised I know your secret?" Prime Mover taunted.

"You were inside She-Devil for at least an hour," said Retaliator. "I could uncover every secret of the Law Legion if I had ten unguarded minutes with the central computer. I imagine it might have taken you twenty."

"Where are your friends, Eric?" said Prime Mover, pressing the pistol more tightly to his temple.

"It's just you and me this time," said Retaliator.

The chief justice's left eye twitched. While his expression of satisfied smugness didn't change, Retaliator knew that Prime Mover had to be disappointed by this news. No doubt he hoped to possess a more powerful hero, someone like—

A circular hole in the roof vanished as a concentrated blast of energy tore apart its molecules. The bright red form of Atomahawk streaked down from the sky, landing in the middle of the room, his fists wreathed with balls of white plasma. He stood with his back to Retaliator, facing the chief justice.

Retaliator started to scream a warning.

He got out the word "close" when the gun at the chief justice's temple disintegrated as Atomahawk's atomavision ripped it apart at a subatomic level.

The word "your" ripped from his throat as the chief justice smiled.

The word, "eyes" crossed his lips as Atomahawk whirled around, now wearing the very same smile.

"Shit," said Retaliator.

"Language," said Prime Mover as he floated into the air, flexing Atomahawk's fingers as if testing to see how well they fit.

Retaliator reached for the anti-space grenade, a small box the size of a deck of cards that could destroy all matter within a three foot sphere by creating a pocket of alternate physics where the Higg's Boson had no mass.

His fingers never reached his belt before Atomahawk's impossibly hot fingers closed around his throat and jerked him from his feet.

"This is more like it," Prime Mover giggled. "The power of a living sun at my command! I'm going to kill a lot of people in the next sixty minutes, Eric. You, however, will not be one of them. You've humiliated me so often, Eric, that I don't want your misery to ever end, Eric, Eric, Eric! When you learn what I've done to…"

Suddenly Atomahawk jerked backward, gasping as if he'd been stabbed. Retaliator fell from his slack grasp, landing, appropriately enough, on the prone form of Vance Davis, the attorney who'd been prepared to argue Prime Mover's case.

Witness floated behind Atomahawk, his ghostly forearm reaching into the radioactive Indian's back. Retaliator could tell from the position of the boy's arm that his fingers were closed around Atomahawk's heart. Prime Mover was getting a full dose of the graveyard touch.

If Witness could distract Atomahawk for another thirty seconds…

It took only three seconds for Atomahawk's reddish skin to flash through every color of the spectrum, then beyond. His skin turned clear as glass. Sparks leapt from the silver buckles on Retaliator's boots. Witness wailed, then disappeared.

Atomahawk fell to his knees as his skin returned to its normal hue. He chuckled breathlessly for a few seconds. "I always… suspected… there was an electromagnetic frequency… that could reach the bloody ghoststream," Prime Mover said, wiping his lips.

"You sound winded," said Retaliator.

"Perhaps I'll massage your heart and see how you sound," Prime Mover grumbled.

"I was going to blame the smoking," said Retaliator, holding up the pack of unfiltered Camels he'd swapped on Atomahawk's utility belt. In his mind, he counted down six, five, four…

"I'm so sorry, John," he said, despite the lump in his throat.

"What are you—"

Prime Mover never finished his sentence. There was a silent flash. In the aftermath, there was a perfectly concave indention in the marble floor where Atomahawk had knelt.

He'd just killed his worst enemy and best friend with a single act, but he had no time to contemplate what had just happened. The goons in the warehouse, with the helicopters and the high explosives—this had never been their target. In the pit of his stomach, he knew where the Prime Mover had sent them.

ERIC GRAY, the man who saw things in black and white, sat amidst the mound of black cinders that had once been his mansion as pure white clouds the shape of comic book thought balloons drifted in the November sky. He had his mask wadded into a ball in his left hand; the island was completely silent. While the place was technically a crime scene, he had enough pull to allow him these few precious, private moments alone in the remains of the house he'd grown up in.

Only, as an even darker shadow fell across the charcoal that had once been the hardwood of his living room floor, he realized that this was no longer a private moment.

"I'm sorry about Nubile," said She-Devil. "Also... well... you know."

"She'll be back," he whispered, through a voice wet with tears. "John, too."

"I understand it's hard to let go," said She-Devil. The outline of her wings and horns were sharply defined as they stretched out before him.

"She's not dead," he said, shaking his head. "We thought she was dead when she was shot. But, she was alive, even if her mind was gone. Now her body's gone. You've played this game long enough. No body, no death. That's how I know Atomahawk will be back, with a story of how he got shunted into another dimension, or backward in time, or whatever. We never stay dead."

She-Devil's shadow horns shook slowly.

"Eric, there's a time when hope is healthy, and a point where it's just a form of self-torture."

Retaliator nodded. "I know a thing or two about torture. There's a pain you can create with despair. And there's a deeper, darker, more desperate pain you can fuel with hope."

Black ash swirled in the chill breeze.

"Things look bleak now," said She-Devil. "You paid a high price. But you won. You finally stopped Prime Mover. He's in hell now. Find comfort in that, if you can."

"You know a lot about hell," said Retaliator.

She-Devil's shadow shrugged. He didn't have the strength to turn his head to face her.

"So you know the myth of Sisyphus."

She-Devil said nothing.

"Condemned to eternally push a rock up a hill. Every time he reaches the top, the stone rolls right back to the bottom."

"I've heard the myth," she said.

"We go out every week and fight bad guys and save the world," said Retaliator. "We die. They die. We all come back. We thwart their plans and lock them in prison cells and two months later they're standing on the Eiffel Tower waving around the latest and greatest doomsday ray, shouting demands. It never ends. It never ends. We get the rock to the top of the hill, and have to watch it roll back to the bottom."

"You're understandably depressed, Eric. You've lost your wife and home. You've lost your best friend. And now the police are hunting Retaliator for the murder of Atomahawk. But you'll bounce back. You'll make it to the top of the hill again. You always do. Maybe this time, the rock will stay put."

Eric rolled his mask into a cylinder and worried it back and forth in his fists. He swallowed his tears, then said, "You told us that you'd been tasked by Satan to find the most wicked men who ever lived and punish them."

She-Devil's shadow froze.

His voice dropped to a near whisper as he asked the question that terrified him most. "Is this… is this hell? Am I Sisyphus? Is this how you've chosen to punish me?"

He turned to see her face.

She was no longer there.

He dropped his mask, as tears streamed down his cheeks. His hands shook as he unsnapped the pouch on the front of his belt. The pouch held an antique, ivory-handled derringer that had belonged to his great-grandfather. Atomahawk had teased him about keeping the relic in his belt along all his high tech toys and gizmos. If he had to carry a gun, certainly Retaliator could have afforded something with a bit more heft.

But it doesn't require that much force to drive a lead slug through the roof of one's mouth. The steel barrel was cold as ice against his lips, and brought forth the most exquisite and horrifying sense of deja vu.

He wondered, when this all began again, if he would remember pulling the trigger.

SECRET ORIGINS

I always found it unsatisfying that superheroes bounce back from death unchanged by the experience. At one point, every single member of the Justice League had been dead a time of two, but I never saw the scene between characters where they said, "Hey, the last time I saw you was at a funeral. You were in the casket."

Of course, after writing this story where I examine the hell of characters not being able to die, I decided not to let these characters die. I wrote a novel called *Cut Up Girl*, where Retaliator, She-Devil, Atomahawk, Golden Victory, and Tempo all put in guest appearances. Oh, Fan Boy's in it too. In the end, I couldn't resist the temptation to keep them alive.

PERHAPS THE SNAIL
ဢ⚬Ꮸ᠙ᏨᏲᏲᏬᏨᏲᏲᏨᏲᏲᏨᏲᏲᏬᏨᏲ

DEVI STOOD BY the giant steel doors that led to the rear parking lot and the band busses. She waited in the sweltering backstage darkness, describing the pre-concert action by phone to her friend Martha. The doors swung open.

"Oh my God," Devi said. "I see him. He's coming up the stairs now. I gotta go."

Martha's reply was cut short as Devi stuffed the phone into her purse. She could see him! Light that had touched Dirk Sinister of the Four Horsemen was even now caressing her retinas and she wondered for a moment if her impending faint would catch his attention or just freak him out.

She clenched her fists and inhaled. She would not faint. That was all there was to it. She'd won the radio contest and had every right to be backstage, basking in Dirk's glow, and she was even due an introduction, once that hag DJ Rosie got out of the toilet.

Dirk loomed exactly as tall as Devi had imagined him to be, as tall as God, and twice as beautiful. He wore a white tuxedo and had his back turned to her, showing off his second face, which yawned and rolled its eyes.

She'd begged her dad to lend her the money for a second face, but he was just an utter bastard about such things. Now, standing in Dirk's presence, she felt glad she hadn't had the implant. It might have looked too derivative, even desperate. No, she would meet Dirk the way God had made her, plus a few accessories, like her "fuck-me-now" silver blouse and her "I-won't-resist" zipper-skirt. She'd changed her hair color about nine times in as many days but had finally settled on a neon blue that matched her panties and Martha had assured her that her make-up made her look like a complete slut.

At last Rosie showed up again. Rosie had always sounded cool on the radio but in person she was like, thirty or something, with a nose three times too big for her face.

"Excited?" Rosie asked for about the ninth time that night.

"Bored," Devi said, despite her fluttering heart. "Wasn't this supposed to get started five hours ago?"

"I think they had some trouble with the moshers," Rosie said. "One of them chewed off his arm trying to escape."

"There's no pleasing some people," Devi said. Moshers would line up for days to get into the pit, and now that it was time to put the chains on they'd try to break free? Devi suspected that she was perhaps the last sane, intelligent person on the planet, with the exception of Dirk.

His songs made it clear that he understood her plight. The first time she'd heard "You Fucking Morons" on the radio, her world became a little less lonely. When she'd downloaded the album, she discovered that "YFM" was only a little sliver of polished glass on a necklace of true gems. Why did radio stations never play the good songs, ones like "Die God Die" or "Snail Love?"

Especially "Snail Love," her favorite, though it was hard to make out the words and the Horsemen never published lyrics. To her it sounded like Dirk sang, "perhaps the snail's an Arab tugged into the boys that ride the whirl," but Martha thought the song said, "perhaps this nail's a scab torn into the voice inside the world." Lyric sites offered a dozen other variants. Whatever the words, they were beautiful. She'd spent countless sleepless nights with the song blaring in her headphones, puzzling it out, piecing it together, decoding Dirk's secret message. The day she solved it, the day she finally knew and understood the words, her life would change forever. She would be wise.

And now the world's only other intelligent person was walking toward her. He was carrying the snail! The heart and soul of the Horsemen sound! Then he yelled something like, "Whoo I'm in love!" and she felt very lightheaded and weak but fainting was *not* on the agenda.

"Where are my gloves?" he shouted again, now just an arm's length away, though he hadn't bothered to look at her yet.

A short bald guy ran up behind Dirk, yelling, "Got 'em!"

"Dirk," Rosie said. "This is Devi Donaldson, the Riot 93.5 concert VIP."

"Oh, God," Devi blurted out. "I'm your biggest fan!"

Her stomach twisted and lurched when she heard her voice. She sounded so juvenile, so *gah gah gah*.

Dirk just stared at her.

"You want I should hold your snail while you glove up?" the short guy asked.

"Sure, Benny," Dirk said, handing him the snail.

He had spoken. In her presence, in her face practically. So close that tiny particles of his breath aroma could lock like microscopic jigsaw pieces into soft moist tissues in her nose if she inhaled, but she couldn't. She just watched as he pulled those white silk gloves over his long slender fingers and tried not to look at his eyes, which were still fixed on her.

"Devi, huh?" he said. "You'll do. Meet me after the show. Benny will let you into my trailer."

Okay, so the fact that she was hearing these words meant that she had, indeed, fainted, and was right now missing her chance to meet Dirk Sinister. The best she could hope for at this point was that she wasn't drooling.

"Dirk," Rosie said. "My boss will probably not be cool with that. We don't need another lawsuit."

"Bennie," said Dirk. "Pay this person to shut up and go away."

"Hah!" said Rosie, as if suddenly getting the joke.

Bennie pulled a thick roll of hundred dollar bills from his back pocket.

"Jesus," said Rosie.

"Get yourself a nose job or something," said Benny.

Rosie took the money, then turned to Devi, "You don't have to do anything you don't want to do."

Devi nodded. This whole thing was happening on some higher level now, something above and beyond a dream, beyond insanity, a sort of hypersanity where her inner will reshaped reality. *Of course* she would be with Dirk Sinister after the show. Rumor had it he was a total sex maniac who would probably force himself on her and subject her to unspeakable depravities. *With any luck.*

Rosie walked away and so did Dirk. Devi trembled.

"You can watch from the wings," Benny said. "I'll come get you when it's time. Dirk will want you in the trailer ready to go."

"I need to sit down now," Devi said, and so she did, landing on her ass with a solid thud. The cement floor beneath her felt warm and slick. She fanned the front of her blouse in and out to cool herself. Her whole body was as wet as if she'd stepped out of a shower.

"You need some water? A beer, maybe?" asked Benny.

"Sure."

Benny disappeared for a while and she watched all the other people milling about, dozens of roadies and techies and hangers-on. Amidst it all she caught a glimpse of Roger the Hammer Fiend mounting his horse, which meant the concert was finally ready to start.

The lights went out as Benny handed her a bottle of water. There was a roar in her head, but also outside her head. The cheers of the audience sounded like the surf of some distant, invisible ocean. She rubbed the cool bottle across her forehead.

Light flooded the stage.

Johnny Rage, the lead motorcyclist, kicked his motor into a low bass drone. Roger the Hammer Fiend pranced his horse to the edge of the stage, the spotlights gleaming on his stainless steel armor. He raised his silver hammer. The crowd roared louder than ever, louder even than the amplified wailing of the chained moshers in the symphony pit.

Dirk Sinister walked on stage. The crowd howled until the walls trembled, until it seemed as if the terrible pressure of their voices would topple the arena walls and rend the earth asunder.

Dirk stepped to the microphone and held out the snail. The snail, the size of a lemon, with a gleaming white shell and moist, vivid-pink flesh, undulated on the video monitors overhead.

The motorcycle backfired. The horse leapt into the air. Dirk lowered the snail onto the microphone.

And then there was noise. The motorcycle accelerated to a treble scream. Roger the Hammer Fiend and his horse landed in the symphony pit, and began to trample and smash the moshers, who wailed their haunting music into his hammer. And above it all was the feedback from the microphone as the snail slid slowly over its surface.

Dirk lowered his lips to the microphone and shouted some lyrics, but by this point Devi had her hands over her ears from the pain. She couldn't tell what he was saying, and without the words it was difficult to identify the song. She had to admit, to her shame, that her father was right about one thing. Melody-wise, all Horsemen songs sounded alike.

Still, he was wonderful to watch, even if she couldn't understand him. Dirk was a gorgeous man, with his lean, long body and those dark-as-space eyes. And Lord help her, his mouth was like the mouth of Jesus, a wholly divine mouth, a mouth from which sprung great truths and secrets, a mouth powerful enough to create her world, her tiny happy secret world. Very soon, she would find out how that mouth felt. Very soon, she would find out how it tasted.

Any faintness left her. She felt completely in control now, the last intelligent woman on the planet. This was *her* reality, and she had plans. She was going to fuck Dirk Sinister so completely he would never forget her, never forgive her. She would do for him what he had done for her, which was destroy any hope of ever having a good night's sleep due to the longing, the need, the desire.

She rubbed the water bottle across her forehead again. The backstage air felt thick and radiant, like sunshine even here in the shadows. She worried briefly about how sweaty she'd grown. But Dirk would be wet, too, after the show. She watched him dancing franticly in the spotlight, beads of light spraying from his faces as he jerked from pose to pose. She ran her hand down her neck, so drenched. She imagined it was his warm hand that touched her. She groaned, inaudible over the din of music. She let her hand trace along her breast, slowly, slipping ever lower, along her bare midriff. She pulled up her skirt. She felt the heat of her crotch with her fingertips long before she touched the soaked cloth of her panties. She felt dizzy and drunk as she ran her fingers along the soft folds of skin beneath the cloth. With a dreamy sigh, she pulled her hand away and took a drink of water. It was so unsatisfying. Her thirst would only be slaked when she drank from Dirk's body.

She lost track of the time, drifting deeper into her fantasies, until someone knelt down next to her. She jerked the hem of her skirt down with a start. It was Benny. She could barely see him in the darkness, and hearing him was out of the question, but he seemed to want her to follow him.

They exited through a metal door into the cool, damp night. From the smell of the air, a thunderstorm had passed recently. The noise level dropped considerably as the door closed behind them. Her ears felt numb and useless. She couldn't hear her footsteps on the steel stairs. A convoy of motor homes waited in the parking lot. Benny led her to a large black one and unlocked the door.

She stepped into Dirk's lair and her head swam. A huge terrarium sat in the center of the room, filled with large snails crawling over rich green foliage. It looked a scene transported straight from the center of a rain forest, and the room smelled like she imagined the jungle would smell, musky and humid, with touches of exotic spice. Flowers twined through the room, in strange shapes and colors, gleaming beneath ultraviolet grow lamps. At the rear of the room was a couch, and across from that a huge bed, covered with animal skins.

"Martha will never believe this," she said. Her voice sounded very far away.

"Okay kid, here are the rules," Benny said, barely audible. "One, don't talk."

"Don't talk?" she said, stretching her jaw from side to side to make her ears pop.

"Jesus, you must be thick," Benny said. "You want to make it with Dirk?"

She nodded.

"Don't talk. If there's anything important to be said, Dirk will say it. Rule two, don't touch him."

She wrinkled her brow in confusion.

"Yeah, yeah, he'll be touching you. But don't touch him. Dirk doesn't go for aggressive. Basically, just take what he gives you. And for God's sake, no moaning. Understand?"

Devi wondered if this was a joke. Benny was certainly making Dirk sound like some kind of weird pervert. Could this night go any better?

"Understand?" Benny asked, sounding miffed.

She nodded.

"Good," said Benny. "Take off your clothes and I'll get you prepared."

"*Ew*," she said.

"You're talking," Benny said.

"You are *not* going to 'get me prepared.' You think I'm stupid?"

"Sure," said Benny. "But don't take it personal."

"Fuck you."

"No, Dirk's the one you want, remember? Jesus, I gotta explain everything? Now listen, I'm serious about this preparation bit. Dirk wants you in a particular pose. He's going to have guests."

"Guests?"

"Don't worry about it. Just take off your clothes. You got maybe ten minutes before the set's over."

"Tell me more about these *preparations*."

"Basically, you take off your clothes, kneel on the bed, I put a tray on your back, some wine, some glasses, and you hold real still for the next hour or so."

"You're joking."

"I don't get paid for comedy," Benny said.

Devi took a deep breath. Time was running out. Maybe Benny was a pervert, maybe Dirk was. One possibility grossed her out, but the other was unquestionably arousing. She nodded, then unzipped her skirt.

"Going for it, huh?" said Benny. "Let's have a little refresher. Two rules. Don't talk. Don't touch. Oh, wait, rule three. Don't look at him. Any questions?"

"One," said Devi.

"Holy shit, is this too complex for you?"

"I get the rules," she said. "But, since you hang out with the band, I was wondering if, um, you might know the words to 'Snail Love?'"

He did. So he told her.

Later, on her hands and knees, a cold silver tray balanced on her back, she realized that she liked her version of the lyrics better.

As Benny opened the door to leave, the sounds of explosions could be heard.

"Final number," he grunted. "Almost show time, kid."

The door closed behind him. *Show time.* She'd planned to give her ultimate performance tonight. She just hadn't counted on being cast as furniture. But, if she had to be a table for someone, at least she would be Dirk's table, if just for one night.

Still, the feeling of control was wearing off. Her sense of hyperreality was melting into surreality. Was she a girl or a table? Was there a difference in the grand scheme of things? She felt as if some deep philosophical truth lay just beyond her grasp.

Then the door opened and Dirk sauntered into the room, followed by a group of men and women with cameras. Devi held very still. Bennie hadn't mentioned reporters, had he?

There was a cacophony of voices.

"Dirk, what about… ?"

" — blames you for the suicide — "

"Senator Walton says that your practice of Satanism is — "

Dirk cut the reporter off. "Practice? Why would *I* need to practice?"

Everyone in the room laughed, except for Devi, who concentrated on not looking at Dirk. Not moving, not making a sound, was real work. Like a mystic rite, an initiation, it required all her strength and will. She reached deep inside to touch her inner table.

But Dirk kept moving closer.

"Actually," Dirk said in response to a follow up question, "the whole Satanism thing is wearing thin. The cattle-like mass of humanity can't imagine the world as anything more than a playing field for two forces, the dark and the light. It takes a mind of infinite compass to grasp the more subtle nature of reality."

Dirk began to disrobe, as the cameras clicked away.

"Who among you can hear the joy and love in the drip of blood falling from a cut wrist onto linoleum? How many of you have listened to the death and darkness tangled up in the laughter of a child?"

Dirk held out his snail as his pants fell to his ankles. From the corner of her eye, Devi could see his enormous erection. Dirk had said in interviews that his performances aroused him. Even now, Dirk was performing. Then she realized that Dirk's second face had its eyes focused on her. She stared at the mattress, taking a slow, deep breath. Dark spots stained the sheet where her sweat rained.

"This snail," Dirk said, turning it slowly in the dim light, "reveals all the secrets of the universe, if you have but eyes to see."

"What species of snail is that?" someone asked.

"My God, what a dreary life you must lead," Dirk said. "Does anyone have an interesting question?"

"What is the secret of the universe?" someone asked, and several people chuckled.

"Am I the only intelligent being in this room?" answered Dirk.

He turned from them and walked to Devi. He placed the snail on the back of her neck. It was warm and wet, like a kiss. As Dirk poured himself a wine, the kiss began to crawl. The reporters continued to babble, but Devi paid no mind. She was trapped inside her body now, focused on the tiny patch of skin that held the snail. The raspy, slick weight undulated slowly around the curve of her neck, toward her throat.

"Noise and pain and sex and magic," Dirk said, distantly. "And now, ladies and gentlemen, if you'll excuse me, I intend to partake in all four."

Dirk climbed onto the bed behind her. The glasses on her back swayed and tinkled. Sweat stormed from her body, darkening the sheet. The cameras kept snapping even as Benny pushed the reporters to the door.

Dirk's hands clasped her hips. Molten steel could not be as hot as those hands. She felt herself melting from the inside, could feel her vital moisture flowing in response.

His cock gently touched her ass and she shuddered, violently clanking the glasses on the tray. She froze, fearing she had offended him. But his hands continued to burn into her hips, and his penis traveled slowly downward, teasing across her slick asshole, continuing down toward the fountain of her moisture. His penis lingered there, barely touching her swollen lips.

The snail reached the dip where her throat joined her chest and hung there like a pendant. As she breathed, she felt its weight. This was magic. This was sex. And she couldn't wait for the noise, and the pain.

Benny pushed the last reporter out and closed the door behind him.

She was alone with Dirk Sinister.

She waited in grand longing for his cock to push into her, to open her, to fulfill her.

Instead, Dirk rose with a grunt, grabbed the bottle of wine from her back, and loped across the room. He slumped onto the sofa and began to drain the bottle.

Devi trembled, suddenly cold. Had she done something wrong? Had she broken a rule?

"Christ," Dirk said. "Look at you."

She turned her head slightly to look at him, remembered rule three, and turned back.

Dirk chuckled joylessly.

"You would do anything, wouldn't you?" Dirk said. "If Benny had produced a razor and told you to shave your head, you wouldn't have hesitated."

Devi didn't know if she should answer. She wanted to assure him that this was indeed the case, that nothing he could ask was off limits. But, remembering rule one, she allowed herself only to nod, ever so slightly. The snail began to creep across her clavicle.

"And what if I were to want something more? What if I asked you to bleed for me? Suppose I smashed this bottle and had a go at your pretty little face?"

Pretty! He thought her face was pretty! But what if he did cut her? She felt her eyes moisten. She didn't know if she was ready for that. She didn't know if she could refuse him.

"Go on," he said. "Screw the first rule. Answer me."

"*Anything*," she said, her voice cracking. "I'm yours."

As she said this she felt something empty grow inside her. It was as if her soul had fled her body, and was even now being inhaled by Dirk. His face bore a little half-smile, as if he enjoyed the taste.

"Do anything you want to me," she groaned.

"I already have," he said. "Put your clothes on. Go."

It took several long seconds for the meaning of these words to register.

"But—"

"I'm done. You're no longer needed. I've already got the bottle." He sloshed the wine back and forth.

"You're not going to fuck me?"

"Haven't I?"

She jerked upright, sending the tray and glasses crashing across the floor.

"What?" she hissed.

He rolled his eyes.

The snail crawled over her left breast above her heart, which had stopped beating. Her mind flashed into rage.

"You prick!" she screamed. "You aren't man enough to fuck me! You aren't—"

She stopped abruptly as he brought up his hand from behind the couch cushion, holding a pistol.

"Fun's over," he said, cocking it.

She cringed, not so much from the gun as from the terrible blackness of his eyes. His eyes held the darkness of the valley of the shadow of death, and she stood in that shadow, in the terrible cold, aware that the breath she was drawing could be her last.

"Oh Jesus don't kill me," she whimpered.

"Get out of my sight. Ten seconds. Nine."

"I don't know where my clothes are."

He grabbed his tuxedo jacket from the back of the couch and tossed it to her feet.

"Six."

She grabbed the jacket and raced toward the door. She paused before opening it, struggling to pull the jacket on. Her arms couldn't find the sleeves.

"Two."

She pushed the door open, stumbling naked into gray drizzle.

She pushed the door shut as the gun went off.

She shrieked.

She stopped.

She wasn't hit.

But with her eyes closed it didn't matter. With her eyes closed it was exactly as if she'd died. She fell to her knees, cold and weak. Her life had ended and she had the opportunity to judge it, to weigh it, to see its true value, which was nothing. Nothing at all. Her life had been like the lyrics of a Horsemen song—utterly meaningless.

Only, this wasn't the end. Her knees stung where she'd hit the pavement. The rain chilled her bare skin. The snail still clung to her, heavy and ticklish as it crept across her ribs. She started to giggle. She opened her eyes, wiped her cheeks with the back of her hand, and gasped for breath. She felt drunk, better than drunk. She felt fucking *alive*.

Benny came up to her, carrying her clothes and purse. He looked tired and old in the dreary light.

"I called you a cab," he said, handing the bundle of belongings to her.

"Oh my God," she said, still giggling. "Oh. My. God!"

"Yeah, yeah," said Benny.

Later, as she waited in the rain for the cab, wearing only Dirk's jacket, she vacated hyperreality, slipped out of surreality, shook off her introspection, and settled into here and now. Here and now, her body vibrated with unspent energy. Here and now, she felt horny. And so, on the wet city street corner, she slipped her hand into the folds of Dirk's long silken jacket and dipped her rain-moist finger between her slippery, swollen lips. She could smell him so strongly, could feel his heat in the fabric, and his kiss was still with her, now tracing a long slick line across her belly toward her shaven mound. Dirk Sinister had tried to kill her, but she was still alive, and she was forever bonded to him because of this. As the snail reached her hand and climbed onto her wrist, she knew she was about to cum.

At that moment, the cab pulled to the curb. The bubble of sexual energy within her popped prematurely as the cabby beeped his horn.

She climbed in and gave her address. The thin, scar-faced cabby had an eye-patch and a hook for a hand. He wore a black and white pinstriped uniform, like some old movie convict. He snarled an acknowledgement to her directions and ground the gears, lurching the cab forward.

She leaned against the window. In the shifting light she examined the snail, now perched upon her finger like a wedding ring. The curves and swirls of the shell encompassed all that had happened to her, all that would ever happen to her. The great spiral of life stood revealed.

She dipped her hand inside the coat and touched herself once more.

With her other hand she found her phone and called Martha.

"What happened?" Martha said. "Was it great? Did you get to talk to Dirk?"

"Yeah," she said, drawing her breath in as she spread her legs wider and slipped further down into the seat. She rubbed her palm over her hairless mound, luxuriating in her own smoothness. "I got to talk to Dirk."

"Oh God. Oh God! Tell me everything."

"Well, for one thing, I found out the words to 'Snail Love.'"

The cabby's one good eye watched in the mirror. Devi tugged the sensitive folds of her labia, spreading them, letting the air touch every part of her. The snail crept from her fingers onto her moist slit. Devi bit her lip.

"Dirk told you? Oh God, Dirk told you the words to one of his songs? I would have died!"

"Perhaps the snail is Ahab," Devi said, "towed into the void astride the whale."

Martha was silent.

"Also," said Devi, arching her back as the snail crept gently along, climbing toward her swollen clit, "I got invited into his trailer where we almost had sex." She felt a small spasm of pleasure ripple up her spine.

"Right," said Martha.

"And then he, like, pulled a gun on me." She began to gently roll the pearl of her clitoris between her soaked fingers as the snail drew ever closer.

"Did you pick up a program?"

"Um," said Devi. She sighed as a wave of warmth washed across her skin. "It slipped my mind."

"You are such a fucking moron," Martha said.

"There were pictures," Devi said, breathing heavily, the eyestalks of the snail now at her fingertips.

"You sound wasted," Martha said. "You home yet?"

"Almost. Almost there." She closed her eyes and pulled her hand away, luxuriating in the unthinkable act about to occur.

"I'll talk to you tomorrow then. You sound like you could use some sleep."

"I may never sleep again..." Her voice trailed off. Her body trembled. She could feel how wet the seat beneath her had grown. The snail crept over her engorged clit, engulfing it with its raspy foot.

"So you're serious?" asked Martha.

"Yes!" she cried, her legs clasping tightly around the shell.

"Those are really the words?"

"Oh God yes!" she screamed as her eyes rolled back in their sockets.

"Christ, they aren't that great."

Devi fell limp. She plunged her hand between her coat and peeled the snail away from her too-tender flesh. She brought it to her lips, and kissed its smooth shell, slick and wet. The snail's long eyestalks swayed gently. In the mirror, she could see the cabby's open mouth. She adjusted the phone, which had slipped from its perch on her shoulder.

"You're right about the lyrics," she said with a sigh. "Kind of a let down, huh?"

"I guess. I dunno," said Martha. "What's a hab?"

"I didn't ask," said Devi, rubbing the shell across her cheek. "It wouldn't matter."

"Wouldn't matter?"

"I decided tonight that meaningless things are beautiful." The snail's eyestalks fluttered across her eyelashes and she giggled.

"The thought seems to please you," said Martha.

"Everything's meaningless," said Devi placing the snail in the center of her brow like a third eye. With it she could see so clearly, from the stars to the cities to the sea, a vast, pretty, pointless world, that no one had crafted for her safety or pleasure. She blew the cabby a pouty kiss. Her hand moved once more to her crotch.

The cabbie wiped the sweat from his eye with his hook as his hand fell to his lap. Devi could hear his fly being unzipped, his breath quickening. They drove into the night, with no one's hand on the wheel.

SECRET ORIGINS

Author Carrie Vaughn was a classmate at the Odyssey Fantasy Workshop. After that, we were part of a mailing list where we would critique the stories of other Odfellows. One day, Carrie posted a snippet of dialogue she'd heard in real life: "You want me to hold your snail while you glove up?" and challenged us to write a story around it. I took the bait.

One part of this story feels a little dated now, and that's Devi's obsession with discovering the words to a song. Today, you can Google any song lyric in 30 seconds. I went to college in pre-internet days, and trying to figure out the lyrics of some songs was a real challenge. I would be hearing the lyrics one way, a friend would be hearing them another way, and when we finally learned the real words, they were almost never as good as what we'd imagined.

This story is a bit of an oddity in my catalog, with no real speculative fiction elements. But, this story captures the nihilist underpinnings of my worldview. Life is utterly pointless, completely meaningless. We are nothing but a brief organization of molecules that will rapidly fall apart and become other things.

And the thought makes me happy. It makes me spread my arms wide as I stare up at a starry skies and gape at the vastness of it all, blissful that, while I may be only a tiny, temporary speck in the ocean of space and time, I'm a speck that's here, now.

In the end, here and now isn't a bad place to be.

About the Author

James Maxey was warned by his mother that if he kept reading so many comic books, it would warp his mind. She was right. James grew into an adult who can't control his daydreaming. Unfit for real work, James ekes out a living typing his depraved fantasies. Parents, if you want to frighten your own children away from such a sad path, feel free to use his blog, dragonprophet.blogspot.com, as a cautionary tale.

Books by James Maxey

SUPERHERO NOVELS
Nobody Gets the Girl
Burn Baby Burn

BITTERWOOD SERIES
Bitterwood
Dragonforge
Dragonseed
Dawn of Dragons

DRAGON APOCALYPSE SERIES
Greatshadow
Hush
Witchbreaker

STEAMPUNK NOVEL
Bad Wizard

Made in the USA
Columbia, SC
04 May 2019